MURDER

MURDER

A NOVEL BY

PARNELL HALL

DONALD I. FINE, INC.

NEW YORK

Library of Congress Catalogue Card Number: 87-81424
ISBN: 1-55611-058-8
Manufactured in the United States of America
10 9 8 7 6 5 4 3 2 1

Library of Congress Cataloging-in-Publication Data

Hall, Parnell.
Murder.

I. Title.
PS3558.A37327M8   1987   813'.54   87-81424
ISBN 1-55611-058-8

For Jim and Franny

1

I'M DOING IT again.

I swore I'd never do it again. I threw my beeper in the Hudson River. I unpacked my briefcase and stuck it in the hall closet. I sent my suit to the cleaners, got it back, and left it wrapped in plastic. And yet, here I am, doing it again. I'm back chasing ambulances for Richard Rosenberg for ten bucks an hour and thirty cents a mile.

You see, something happened.

What happened was, Tommie went to kindergarten.

If that doesn't make any sense, perhaps I should say, Tommie went to *private school* kindergarten.

Now I know I'm an old fogy, and times have changed and there's inflation and all that, but still, Tommie's kindergarten costs three times what it cost me to go to college.

It was harder to get into, too. First Tommie had to pass the ERB's. Last year, Tommie was evaluated by examiners who came around to his nursery school and administered aptitude tests. My wife and I sweated out the results for a month and a half before finding out that Tommie had scored above average in both English and math. At age four, for Christ's sake.

Then we applied to kindergarten. We applied to six since competition in New York City is fierce. Each application carried a nonrefundable fee of anywhere from twenty to thirty-five dollars. Each application form had long essay questions such as, "Describe your child's strengths and weaknesses, and explain why you feel he or she would be well-suited to function in our school environment." Despite the fact that the same paragraph, slightly altered, could fit all forms, needless to say, after the first few applications my wife and I were nervous wrecks.

The letters came in February. Tommie was accepted by two schools, rejected by one, and put on three waiting lists!

All of this affected Tommie not at all. Our relief was boundless.

The school we chose for Tommie was the East Side Day School, a primary school, kindergarten through 6th grade, with 250 students, in a converted apartment building on East 84th Street. Tuition was six thousand dollars a year.

It was my wife who decided that Tommie should go to private school. Her chief argument was that the public school classes were too large for a boy of his temperament. The public school had thirty-two kids in the kindergarten. The East Side Day School has twenty-two kids in the kindergarten. So I figure I'm paying ten kids six hundred bucks a piece not to be in Tommie's class.

Actually, my father-in-law, the renowned plastic bag manufacturer, is kicking in half the tuition, perhaps in the hope that someday Tommie will grow up and take over the family business. That helps tremendously, but it still leaves a three thousand dollar hole to fill.

In the months since quitting my job with Richard, I had done my best to make it as a writer. Despite my wife's presumed opinion (she never actually expresses it, but I am convinced it is what she thinks) that I am timid about meeting people, I actually got out and hustled. I got an interview with a director from a soap opera, which went fairly well, except for the fact that I didn't get any work, and I got a job writing copy for some kid's magazine, which was either "Transformers" or "Gobots," I'm not sure, which gives you some idea of my involvement in the project.

The problem is, I didn't want to write soap operas or children's magazines. I wanted to write books. And more than that, I wanted to write books that got published. And more than that, I wanted to write books someone actually read. When you came right down to it, basically, I wanted to be Kurt Vonnegut.

I saw Kurt Vonnegut's Address to the Graduating Class of 1970 at Bennington College. I didn't go to Bennington college, I went to Goddard, and I didn't graduate in 1970, I'm even older than that, but I was living in Massachusetts at the time and I drove up to Bennington with friends to hear Vonnegut speak.

He was wonderful. A tall man with shaggy hair and a drooping mustache, he stood at the lectern and told us, "It isn't often that a total pessimist is invited to speak in the springtime." The audience ate it up. Of course, he had his prepared text in front of him, and all he had to do was deliver it. And, of course, he had a hell of a speech writer.

I've read "Cat's Cradle" five or six times, "Slaughter-house 5" about that many, "Sirens of Titan" at least three. I wanted to write like that. I thought I *could* write like that. "What's Vonne-gut that I ain't got?" I'd ask myself. The answer, of course, was talent, style, wit, and a career. Seeing as how, "What's Vonne-gut that I ain't got?" was the extent of *my* wit, it's not surprising I didn't get anywhere.

So, with Tommie in kindergarten, I was up against it. And the sad fact was, what with my liberal arts education, there was just no job I was qualified for that was going to pay me *more* than ten bucks an hour and thirty cents a mile. So, after much soul-searching, I capitulated. I took my suit out of plastic, packed up my briefcase, strapped on a new beeper, fired up the ancient Toyota, and now I'm back on the road again, investigating accident cases for the law firm of Rosenberg and Stone. Stanley Hasting, P.I., is back in business.

And I'm mixed up in a mystery again. And, oddly enough, it was Tommie going to kindergarten that got me into that too.

2

"**Y**ou have to help her," my wife, Alice persisted.

My wife has implicit faith in my ability to do things. That is, she has implicit faith that I *have* the ability to do things. I'm afraid she also feels I lack the gumption to *do* them. My wife never actually expresses this opinion, however—it's just what I think she feels, and I'm sure it's all tied up in my own neurotic insecurity and fears, but, nevertheless, that's how I see it. Regardless, I'm sure my wife feels I'm *capable* of anything.

What makes this remarkable is the fact that my wife doesn't know I solved the Albrect murder. In fact, no one knows I solved the Albrect murder. Martin Albrect was a drug courier who got executed for ripping off some of the shipment. I'd kept my involvement in the case strictly in the dark, whether through prudence or fear, you take your pick.

Even without knowing this, my wife was still convinced I could "help her."

The "her" in question was Pamela Berringer, the mother of one of Tommie's classmates. The Berringers lived on the Upper West Side a few blocks from us, and we car-pooled to kindergarten. There was a bus, but it was eleven hundred dollars a year, and the three thousand seemed enough of a burden, thank you very much.

"Help her what?" I asked.

"Get out of a mess," she told me.

"What mess?"

"The mess she's in."

"Oh, that explains it," I said. "Exactly what mess is she in?"

"I'd rather she told you about it."

"Why?"

"I'd just rather she would."

"How can I help her out of this mess if I don't know what it is?"

"She'll tell you about it."

"Why don't you?"

"I don't want to. You're going to have to hear it from her, anyway."

"How do I know if I can help her if I don't know what the problem is?"

"You can help her."

"Yeah. But what if I can't?"

"You can."

"Fine. Great. Thanks for your support. But it's still my decision. What if when I find out what this is all about I decide I can't help her?"

"You won't."

"Yeah, but what if I do?"

My wife threw up her arms and shook her head, smiling in a way that managed to be somewhat endearing and somewhat annoying at the same time. "You won't. I'm telling you you won't. But if that should happen, you just tell her you're sorry, there's nothing you can do."

"That's the problem."

"What?"

"I don't want to do that."

"What do you mean, you don't want to do that? If you can't help her—and that's silly to talk about because it isn't going to happen—but if you can't help her, you just say no, you can't do it."

I shook my head. "No. No good."

"What do you mean, no good? You have the right to say no. That's your big problem. You just don't know how to say no."

"No."

"Very funny."

"I mean it. If I can't help her, I don't want her over here."

"Why?"

"Because I don't want to sit and listen to her tell me a long story about her problem, and then have to tell her there's nothing I can do."

One of the reasons I didn't want to do that was because that was exactly what had happened in the Martin Albrect case. And the next day he was dead.

Of course, my wife didn't know that. "That's silly," she said.

"I don't care if it's silly. That's how I feel about it. If you want me to help her, tell me about it now."

My wife began to squirm a little. "I really don't want to."

"What's the matter," I said. "Is she a hooker, or something?"

My wife's eyelids flicked for a split second before she turned on me. "No, she's not a hooker," she said irritably.

And suddenly I realized, Jesus Christ, she *was* a hooker. She had to be. My wife's reaction was too sharp, too vehement. What she was saying, in effect, was not "She's not a hooker" but "Don't *call* her a hooker." She might as well have said, "She's not a hooker, she's a decent woman who just happened to get involved."

Alice wouldn't say another word on the subject, but it didn't matter. Her protestations notwithstanding, I would have bet my life right then and there that Pamela Berringer, respectable housewife, mother of Tommie's playmate Joshua, and member of our car pool, was turning tricks.

3

PAMELA BERRINGER HAD MARRIED young. After all, she had a kid Tommie's age, and she couldn't have been more than twenty-five or twenty-six. She was of medium height, with a slender, youthful figure. Her shoulder-length dark hair, curling up at the ends, and her button nose, gave her a school-girl look.

She made me feel like an old man.

A dirty old man.

She sat on the couch next to my wife, who seemed to be sitting close to her for moral support. I was sitting in a chair across from them. We'd exchanged hellos. Now we were just sitting. I knew one thing for sure. I wasn't taking the conversational lead.

My wife did. "It's all right, Pamela," she told her. "You can tell him anything."

Pamela looked at me. I must say I felt sorry for her then. She really looked trapped. "It's so hard," she said.

"I know," my wife said, sympathetically. "But Stanley will understand."

I wasn't sure I *would* understand. But I was also sure

15

I'd *never* understand if I didn't hear the story. So I said, "Why don't you tell me about it?"

That seemed to frighten her more. Before I was just an observer. Now I was an interrogator. She had recourse to tears. My wife put her arm around her and patted her shoulder.

I got up, went in the kitchen, and made some coffee. I am admittedly not the best judge of situations, but in my estimation the meeting was not going well. I wasn't sure coffee was the answer, but making it sure beat sitting in that room.

I heated up milk on the stove and made three cappucinos. I put them on a tray with a bowl of sugar and a tin of cinnamon and brought them into the living room, where things seemed to have calmed down somewhat.

"Here we are," I said, putting the tray down on the coffee table. "Cappucino à la Stanley, my one culinary triumph, providing I don't burn the milk. We take it straight, but if sugar is to your taste, I promise not to be offended."

We took the cups, passed around the cinnamon, and took sips. It wasn't bad, considering I'd been somewhat preoccupied while I made it.

"Well," I said, "here we are, a nice Tuesday morning, the kids in school, god bless the car pool, keep the eleven hundred dollars. What could be better?"

Pamela looked at me. Her lower lip trembled, and the corner of her eyes began to glisten.

"On the other hand," I said, "it might well rain."

Tears again started down her cheeks. My wife shot me a dirty look, hugged Pamela again.

I sighed. "O.K., Pamela," I said, plunging in. "Now if I'm going to help you, I gotta hear your story. I'm sorry if that upsets you, but I gotta tell you this. As a private detective, all I do is listen to people's stories. I hear hundreds of them. And the people aren't people to me, they're just clients, and their stories aren't stories, they're just facts, and their problems aren't problems, they're just cases I have to deal with. So telling your story may seem like a big deal to you, but as far as I'm concerned, it's just data."

I felt like adding, "And if you buy that, I have this land in Florida," but I figured that wouldn't be wise.

Pamela blinked at me. "You're really a private detective?"

That was a touchy point for me, since I didn't consider myself a *real* private detective, but I didn't figure it was a good time to debate the point. "That's right," I said. "Wanna see my I.D.?"

She almost smiled. "No."

"O.K. So tell me about it. It all started about fill-in-the-blank time ago when I met blank."

"Yes," she said, surprised, and apparently somewhat relieved. "That's just it. It all started about a year ago when I met this girl I knew in college."

"What's her name?" I asked.

It was a mistake. She drew back into her shell again. "Does it matter?"

I shrugged. "I don't know, 'cause I haven't heard your story yet. You don't want to tell me her name?"

"I'd rather not."

"O.K. You don't want me to know who she is. I understand. But it's going to be kind of confusing keeping everybody straight unless we call her something. So you could use her first name. Unless it's something like Hildegard."

"It's Jane."

"Fine. I doubt if that compromises her anonymity any. So tell me about Jane."

"O.K. Well . . . I guess I better start at the beginning."

"Usually a wise move."

Pamela took a deep breath. "O.K. Well, you see, Ronnie's on the road a lot."

I kept a straight face, but inwardly I groaned. It was a terrible beginning. "Ronnie's on the road a lot." Shit. Maybe I'm just an old fogy, but it was such a damn cliché, and not one that was likely to evoke my sympathy. I could fill in the rest of the story myself. The husband, on the road, traveling for his job. The wife, sitting home alone, bored, restless, looking for something to do.

Jesus.

As usual, I was wrong.

It wasn't that at all.

4

"**W**ELL," PAMELA SAID. "You know how it is. It's hard having Ronnie gone all the time. I mean, I know he has to travel for his job, and we need the money, and all that, but it's still hard.

"So, the thing is, I'm alone a lot. And I don't get out much, I mean what with Joshua, and trying to get a baby-sitter and all that. Well, I'm sure you know all about that."

"We do," I assured her.

"Well, anyway, it was about a year ago. Ronnie was in Chicago, and there was this party I got invited to by one of my girlfriends, and, miracle, I got a baby-sitter and I went."

"And that's when you met Jane," I prompted.

"Yes. Well, I didn't *meet* her there, I knew her from college. Not well, but I knew who she was. We were both at Cornell together. I mean, not together, but at the same time. We had a class together, though. I think it was anthropology. Maybe not. Maybe it was English. I'm not really sure."

"Probably doesn't matter," I suggested.

19

"No, I guess not. No, of course not. Well, anyway, I didn't know her that well, but you know how it is when you meet someone you went to school with. You start reminiscing and swapping stories, and did you know what's-his-face is a doctor and all that. And of course, she asked me what I was doing and I told her I was married and had a kid. And then I asked her what she was doing, and it turned out she had a kid, too. A boy. Three years old. Just a year younger than Joshua was then.

"Well, that was great, you know, because it gave us something to talk about. I mean, we really had nothing in common. But a kid, well, that's a common ground, and I thought, fine, we can chat a bit, just two moms together.

"Only it wasn't like that. See, in the first place she wasn't married. She'd never been married. And if you knew her, that wouldn't surprise you, because she wasn't the kind of girl you would have expected to get married. I mean not the kind of girl any one would have wanted to marry. I don't know how to explain it, really. She wasn't pretty, but she wasn't ugly, either. She just didn't have any spark, you know. Some people do and some people don't. And she didn't. She just wasn't the type of person you could imagine anyone being in love with. From what I gathered, the kid's father was a one night stand. At any rate, he was out of the picture. So it was just her and the kid.

"And the other thing was the kid. It had problems. Down's Syndrome. It was severely retarded and required constant care. Just Jane's luck, somehow. Her medical bills were astronomical. Plus the money she spent on child care. I mean, it's hard enough on a single mother, without all that too.

"So, there I was, starting off on this happy, ain't-it-great-to-be-moms talk, and suddenly I'm caught up in someone's personal tragedy. So, of course, I was very sympathetic, and I asked her how she was managing all that, and she told me."

Pamela paused here, looked down, and seemed to be searching for the right words, and I knew we were getting to it.

We were.

"She told me she worked for an escort service," Pamela said. "She was a paid escort. She went out on dates with men." She looked up again. "It was strange to think of her doing that. I mean, she wasn't pretty, and she didn't have any fire, and she wasn't the type of girl men noticed, you know what I mean. But she's young, my age, and I guess if you put make-up on her, and put her in a dress, well, she's a young girl to some older man. You know?"

"Yeah," I said softly.

Pamela sighed, and her body seemed to shudder. "Well," she said, "that was it. And that was the end of the party, as far as I was concerned. I mean after talking to Jane, I just didn't feel like staying there. I made some excuse or other, left, went to a movie so as not to waste the baby-sitter, and went home."

She paused again and took a deep breath. This was going to be the hard part. She started, haltingly at first, and told the story.

"It was about a month later. I'd more or less forgotten about the incident. Put it out of my mind. And I got a

call from Jane. Which was a shock. I hadn't expected to
hear from her. We hadn't exchanged numbers. She must
have looked me up in the book.

"She was really upset. She was crying, and she
sounded desperate. Her mother had had a heart
attack—wasn't expected to live. She had to catch a
plane, fly to Indiana with her kid. The thing was, her
escort service had booked her a date for that night. If
she didn't keep it, she'd lose her job. That's what she
told me. That's the way she put it. Lose her job. She
was hysterical. She kept saying she'd lose her kid. Lose
her kid. She wouldn't have any money, she couldn't
support him, the state would take him away and put
him in a home. It didn't make any sense, but there was
no reasoning with her."

A pause. Then. "She asked me to cover for her. It was
simple, she said. I just had to put on makeup and a
dress, look pretty, go to this hotel room and wait, and a
man would show up and take me out to dinner."

She paused again. I said nothing. Waited.

"Ronnie was in Atlanta on business. I knew I could
leave Joshua with the neighbors next door. And Jane
was so upset. So upset."

A longer pause. A deep sigh.

"So I did."

A tear started down her cheek. She brushed it away.
Took a sip of coffee.

I glanced at Alice. She was sitting perfectly still, saying nothing.

Pamela put down her coffee cup. The clatter of cup
on saucer was tremendous in that quiet room.

"It was a hotel on East 79th Street. Clean. Respectable. I had to stop at the desk to get my key. They gave

it to me, no questions asked. I went up to my room. It was a nice room. Comfortable. I sat and waited. I'd brought a book along. I sat and read.

"At eight o'clock there was a knock on the door. I got up and answered it.

"It was a man. He looked like a businessman. He had a suit on. He was an older man. Probably in his forties."

I'm forty myself, and under any other circumstances, Pamela Berringer would have considered that a tactless remark, but as things were, she didn't even notice.

"He wasn't attractive. He was fat and ugly. And I didn't want to go out with him, but a deal's a deal, so I smiled at him, and said, 'Where do you want to go?'

"He leered at me. I'll never forget that look in his eyes. He just leered at me, and there was a cruel smile on his lips, and he said, 'Go?' He chuckled and shook his head, and he said, 'Go?'

"And I said, 'Yeah, go. Where do you want to go out to? Where do you want to have dinner?'

"He was laughing now. He said, 'Out? Dinner?' Then he grabbed my arm and pulled me toward the bed.

"I screamed, and tried to twist away. He slapped me across the face. Hard. It stunned me. I was in shock. And afraid. Very afraid. I looked at his face. It was vicious. Cruel, Jesus. I tried to twist away again, but he grabbed the front of my dress, and pulled, and ripped it down the front.

"I grabbed for my dress, to pull it around me, and he hit me again. Slugged me across the face.

"Then he grabbed me and threw me down on the bed, and . . . then he raped me."

Tears were streaming down both cheeks now, and

she was making no effort to stop them. Her shoulders heaved.

Alice put her arm around her. Pamela stiffened at the touch. Shrugged the arm away. It was as if any physical contact was too much for her now.

Pamela wiped her eyes, rubbed her face.

"You wouldn't have thought it could have gotten any worse, but it did. I was lying there, with this pig on top of me, and suddenly there was a flash of light.

"I was so startled, I almost flung him out of bed, all two hundred pounds of him.

"I looked, and there was a man crouched by the bed. A black man. Grinning and holding a flash camera. When I looked up, he took another shot.

"I started screaming. And he walked over to the bed, all cool and deliberate, and he grinned at me, and he said, "Hi. I'm Darryl Jackson." And then he slapped me hard.

"He held up the camera. It was a Polaroid, you know, instant pictures. He held up the two shots he'd just taken, and let me watch them develop. And when they did. When they came out bright and crisp and clear, he grinned again, and he said, "You want these?""

Pamela let out a tremendous sigh.

"I've been working for him ever since."

5

MY BEEPER WENT OFF about then, and, quite frankly, I was glad. Pamela Berringer was sobbing her eyes out, and, even with Alice ministering to her, it looked like it was going to be a good while before we could continue the interview. I excused myself, went in the kitchen, and called the office of Rosenberg and Stone.

During my absence, Richard Rosenberg's two secretaries, Susan the perennially cheery and Kathy the perennially sour, had moved on to greener pastures and been replaced by Wendy and Cheryl, the perennially incompetent. They had similar voices, so I was never sure whom I was talking to. It didn't matter. Whoever it was, the information would invariably be wrong.

"Rosenberg and Stone," came the voice of Wendy or Cheryl.

"Agent double-0-5," I told her. I used to be Agent Blue, but during my sabbatical, the office bookkeeping system had switched over to numerical coding. I was designated "05," but I protested that if I had to have a number, it was damn well going to be a double-0 number, and I wrote "005" on all my paysheets and case folders.

Wendy/Cheryl had a new case for me. I whipped out my pocket notebook and wrote down the info: a Miss Sally Webber of 105 West 141st Street, Manhattan, had fallen down on her stairs and broken her leg, and an appointment had been made for me to see her between 11:00 and 12:00.

I wasn't sure how long this thing with Pamela was going to take, and I also had to swing by Photomat to drop off the accident pictures I'd taken that week, so I decided to push the appointment back to between 12:00 and 1:00.

I called the number I'd been given. I don't know who the guy was who answered, but he sure wasn't Sally Webber, and he'd never heard of her either. I called information, and asked for a listing for a Sally Webber at 105 West 141st Street. There was none, but there was an S. Webber at *150* West 141st Street. I said I'd take it.

I called the number and asked for Sally Webber. She wasn't there, but damned if *Sherry* Webber wasn't, and damned if she hadn't broken her leg and called Rosenberg and Stone. I apologized and pushed the appointment back an hour.

I went back into the living room, where things seemed to have calmed down. To be honest, the beep had been a godsend, giving me an excuse to breeze through the rest of the interview, and I played it for all it was worth.

"O.K.," I said. "That was the office and I gotta go. I stalled 'em some, but I still gotta go, so we're gonna have to cut this down to the bare essentials. Now, if I'm going to help you, I gotta have the facts. So I'm going to ask you specific questions, and I want you to give me specific answers. Try to keep your answers as short as you can. In fact, answer yes or no whenever possible. You understand?"

"Yes."

"Good start. O.K. The black guy who took your picture. He's your pimp?"

She winced at the word.

My wife said, "Stanley!"

I turned to Alice. "Well, that's what he is, isn't he? Whaddya want me to call him, the Master of Ceremonies? Look, she's in trouble and she needs help. We're never gonna get anywhere if we keep pretending her problem is she can't decide what to wear to the junior prom. Now, keep quiet and let me ask my questions."

I'm sure my wife was ready with some terrible rejoinder, but Pamela cut her off.

"He's right," she said. She turned to me. "Yes, he's my pimp."

"Good girl," I told her. "What's his name again?"

"Darryl Jackson."

"Where's he live?"

"Harlem."

"And you've been working for him?"

"Yes."

"On a regular basis?"

"Yes."

"How regular?"

"Five days a week."

"How many times a day?" (Despite the fact she was doing great now, I said times instead of tricks. I didn't want to push it.)

"Three or four."

"What did you charge?"

"A hundred dollars."

"How much did he take?"

"Eighty percent."

I'm afraid I raised my eyebrows.

"Well, I wasn't doing it for the money," she flared. "Sure that's a lot, but—"

"Skip it," I said. "Where was this, up in Harlem?"

"No. I had a room in a hotel. A nice hotel. On East 79th Street."

"The same hotel where—"

"Yes."

"And Duane got you the room?"

"Darryl."

"Right. Darryl."

"Yes."

"And paid for it?"

"Yes."

"And set you up there?"

"Yes."

I tried to phrase this one tactfully. "Did you have to go out, or did he send you people?"

"He sent me people."

"Anyone else use the room? When you weren't there?"

"I don't know. I guess so. I mean, yes, I'm sure they did."

"But you never met them?"

"No."

"Never met any of his other girls?"

"No. Except Jane."

"But he had others?"

"Yes."

"And you went there five days a week?"

"Yes."

"How could you manage that? I mean, how could you get out of the house five nights a week?"

"It wasn't at night."

"No?"

"No. It was in the morning. After I took . . . after I took Joshua to school."

Her lip trembled and we were off again.

"All right, never mind that," I said. I felt cruel as hell, but I really had no choice. If I let her go on we'd be here all day. "You can cry later. Right now I need the facts. The thing is, you wanna get out and this guy won't let you."

"Yes."

"When did you tell him you wanted out?"

"About a month ago."

"What did he say?"

"He laughed at me. He said no one gets out. He's a monster, a sadistic, cold-hearted—"

"I'm sure he is. But the point is, you want to get out."

She stopped. Looked at me. And then laughed, an ironic, bitter laugh. "Yeah," she said. "I want to get out. Listen. Do you know how often I go to the doctor? You wouldn't believe it." She paused and then said, slowly and evenly, "As of last week I do not have AIDS. But I'm scared. I'm so scared."

A chill went down my spine. That part of it hadn't even occurred to me.

"I see," I said. I hated to ask the next question, but I had to. "Tell me, does your husband know about this?"

She was horrified. "No! That's just the point. Ronnie doesn't know. Ronnie must never know."

"I see," I said, and I did. Ronnie must never know. I

must say I felt a little funny about dear old Ronnie. Three or four tricks a day, five days a week for six months added up to three or four hundred separate counts of adultery. In some states that would probably entitle Ronnie to a divorce.

"O.K. I think I got the picture. You want out, and this guy says if you quit he's gonna tell your husband."

Pamela nodded. "Yes." She lowered her head. "And . . ."

Shit! There was an "and."

"And?" Then I remembered. "Oh, yes. The pictures."

"Pictures?"

"The polaroids."

"Oh. Those." She waved them away. "No, I got those back long ago." She lowered her head again. "But . . ."

Jesus. An "and" and a "but."

"But what?"

"He has a tape."

"A tape?"

"A video tape."

"Of you?"

"Yes."

"You mean he had a hidden camera and taped you without you knowing it?"

She lowered her eyes, said softly, miserably, "No."

Jesus.

I was trying hard not to be shocked, but this was a little much. I could grant her the motivation and all that. There'd been coercion. She'd been forced into it. But still. Darryl Jackson hadn't filmed her without her knowledge. She'd *posed* for the dirty pictures. She'd acted for the camera while that sleazeball made his filthy videotape.

Now, I'm not a prude, and I'm not even against pornography. In fact, I like to look at dirty pictures as much as the next guy. But you never really think of the people in dirty pictures as *people*, if you know what I mean. They don't seem real.

But Pamela Berringer was. And somehow her posing for the pictures seemed worse to me than her turning tricks.

It seemed worse to her too. This time there was no stopping the deluge. I managed to worm Darryl Jackson's address and phone number out of her in between sobs. I wrote it in my notebook.

I said I'd see what I could do. I nodded to Alice, who was doing her best to be of comfort, and wished Pamela well.

And got the hell out of there.

6

I was in a foul mood as I drove down to the Photomat. See what I could do, hell! What the hell *could* I do? This guy had the tape and I had to get it. What was I gonna do, walk up and ask him for it? I could offer him money, but that wouldn't work. I hadn't had a chance to ask Pamela how high she'd be willing to go, but whatever it was, it wouldn't be enough. The guy was pulling in over a grand a week from her tricking, so it would take a small fortune to make him give that up. So how could I get the tape? Steal it? I'd have to find it first. How would I go about doing that? Damned if I knew. Trick him out of it? How? Scare him out of it? Fat chance, seeing as how I'm a devout coward who doesn't carry a gun, can't fight, and avoids confrontations.

The other thing was, how did I feel about what I was doing? I mean, Pamela Berringer was obviously someone who needed help. Who deserved help. Hearing her story, I couldn't have felt more sorry for her. Seeing her sitting there, distraught and miserable, pouring her heart out.

But the thing was, as soon as I got out of there, I began to have doubts. I mean, come on. I'm supposed to believe in a girl so naive she doesn't know "escort" is a euphemism? Could I take Pamela's story at face value? The thing is, I'm pretty gullible. I believe what I hear. One of the hardest things about my job is realizing that people don't always tell you the truth. And one of my severe limitations as a private detective is I'm not always sure what's true and what isn't.

The thing is, people always try to make a case for themselves. They always try to put their story in the best light. They always try to justify their actions. They always want you to think well of them. And in this case, could it really be true? I mean, old college chums, dying mothers, and Down's Syndrome, for Christ's sake. Did I have to swallow all that? Was it really true?

Or was it a story made up by a hooker to try to justify herself?

You have to understand how I felt. (Right, screw her moral justifications, here come mine). You see, I consider myself a liberal. On the other hand, I'm forty years old. When I was young, sexual equality was not something I ever particularly thought about. I grew up at a time when mailmen were mailmen, and no one was seriously suggesting they be called mailpersons or even mailcarriers. The women's liberation movement sort of blind-sided me in the late 60's early 70's. I'd never realized I was a male chauvinist pig before. In fact, I didn't even know what chauvinist meant, I had to look it up. But then I bet some of the *persons* calling me it were only really clear on what pig meant. Be that as it may, when confronted with the women's liberation movement, I examined it, saw the truth in it, and adjusted my perspectives. I still don't believe women should be given jobs as firemen if they can't carry people out of burning buildings, and I don't believe the department's standards should be lowered just to give them jobs. But I do believe in equal pay for equal work, and I do believe women have been getting the short end of the stick, which, I just realized, is a horrible way to phrase it under the circumstances.

And, as far as sex goes, I know there's a double standard, and it's not right. And I realize now that women are sexual creatures, just like men, and that they have the same, or at least similar, drives and needs and feelings. I know all that, and I believe it.

Intellectually.

But, to be honest, in my heart of hearts, my feeling about women and sex is just the same as it was way back when I was a horny teenager just looking to get laid. And, with all due apologies to Gloria Steinam et al., it is this: any woman who has sex with me is sensitive, intelligent, perceptive and discerning—any woman who has sex with anyone else is a slut.

Now, as Johnny Carson would say, please don't write in. That's a one-liner, gang, not a moral philosophy. Please note the presence of tongue in cheek. All I'm saying is, liberal protestations notwithstanding, many men have confused and conflicting feelings about women and sex, and sexually active women tend to make them nervous. And the thing is, there is some ancient male instinct that says when you get on your white horse to slay dragons for your damsel in distress, as long as you're risking your life for her, you should be able to think of her as sweet and pure and clean.

Particularly if you're a coward to begin with.

*   *   *

I got a meter on 57th Street between 9th and 10th, and walked over to Broadway to drop off my film at the Photomat. It was crowded, and when I finally got up to the counter, the clerk who waited on me was one I hadn't seen before. He was young, crisp, efficient. He grabbed my five rolls of film, looked at me, and said, "3½ by 5, or 4 by 6?"

"What?" I said.

"What size do you want? 3½ by 5, or 4 by 6?"

"I want the standard size," I told him.

"They're both standard sizes," he said.

I blinked.

"Well," he said, crisply. "I'll fill this out while you decide. Name?"

"Stanley Hastings. I have an account."

"Fine. Address?"

I told him and he wrote it down.

When he'd finished filling out the envelope he looked up at me. "Have you decided what size you want?"

There was nothing particularly offensive in his manner, but still he had managed to convey the impression that I was an idiot who couldn't make up his mind.

If I'd been in a better mood, I'm sure I would have been able to think back to all the thousands of pictures I'd identified for my job, and figure out if they were 3½ or 4 inches tall, and 5 or 6 inches wide. But I wasn't in a good mood, and I didn't feel like thinking about it.

"I want the size I always get," I told him.

His look said, "How would I know what that was?" What he actually said, which I found equally annoying, was, "And what size might that be?"

"All right, look," I said. "I've been dropping off pictures here for years, and this is the first time anyone has ever asked me this question. In light of that, what size pictures have they been giving me?"

"Well," he said. "In that case, they've been giving you 3½ by 5."

"Fine," I said. "Then that's what I want."

I got my film receipts and got the hell out of there. I don't know why the guy irritated me so much. I guess it's just that there are so many simple things in life, and somehow people always manage to make them so complicated. Too many options. Too many choices. And it really wasn't the film thing that was bothering me. It was life in general. The film thing just seemed to set it off.

And I knew it was crazy, what I was thinking, but I couldn't help it, cause I'm human, and you can't help thinking things, even when you know how ridiculous they are. But, you see, I didn't know what Pamela Berringer's story *really* was. Maybe it was just as she said. But maybe not. Maybe she was just bored. Or maybe she heard time's winged chariot drawing near and decided to stop being coy. How the hell should I know? But it certainly wasn't rational to assume she was just a perfectly normal, happy housewife, who would have been just fine if one day a school chum named Jane hadn't come up to her and said, "3½ by 5, or 4 by 6?"

7

I DROVE UPTOWN to see Sherry Webber, and in my mind I played the game I always play in these situations: How bad is it going to be? See, the thing about my job as a private detective is it's pretty routine and pretty dull. The only thing that adds spice to it, if you could call it that, is the possibility I could get killed. That's not because my job itself is particularly dangerous; it isn't. It's just that since many of Richard's clients are economically deprived, I have to go into some pretty bad neighborhoods to see 'em. And I have to wear a suit and tie. Often, this makes me the only white man in a suit and tie in the neighborhood. In my mind that makes me a target. In the minds of the people in the neighborhood, that makes me a cop. As far as I'm concerned, I don't much care if a junkie wants to kill me because he thinks I'm a cop come to bust him or because he thinks I'm a mark with some money—in either case I don't like it.

If you get the idea I'm a coward, you're right. I'm a big coward, and rightfully so. I don't carry a gun or any other means of protection, and if anyone makes a move

37

on me, I'm dead. Frankly, there are some neighborhoods that scare the hell out of me.

I've been on the job long enough that often just the
street address will tip me off to an undesirable neighborhood. Or sometimes the facts of the case will—for
instance, if a girl was raped because the back door of
her building is unlocked and she lives next door to a
methadone clinic, it's sort of a dead giveaway I won't
be enjoying my visit.

But sometimes the street address and the case info
tells me nothing, and I have to go to the Hagstrom map
and look it up. Sometimes the index itself is enough—
map 11, grid F-13 or 14 is apt to be a fairly bad section
of Bedford Stuyvesant/East New York. Sometimes I
don't know until I turn to the actual page, and sometimes I don't know even then, and won't know until I
get there.

But always in my mind I play the game: how bad is it
going to be?

In Sherry Webber's case I wasn't sure. West 141st
Street is Harlem, but there's Harlem and there's *Harlem*, if you know what I mean. I couldn't remember
anything in the 140's as far east as the West 100 block.
Let's see, 141st was fairly high for Harlem; did that put
it in the Washington Heights area? Could be. I don't
know if it runs that far east. There are no definite
boundaries, at least none that I know. So how bad was
it?

The thing that added fuel to my paranoia was all the
recent furor about crack. God, I wish they'd stop these
drug innovations. I'd just about figured out what freebase was, when suddenly there was crack, which I
gather is sort of like freebase only you don't have to do
it yourself, sort of instant freebase. Anyway, the media

had gone wild on the stuff. Every day I'd pick up the paper and see "Killer Crack." Sometimes it would be "Crazed Crack Killer." The articles were all the same, usually about some junkie who killed someone for twenty bucks cause he just had to have a couple of hits of crack. Well, I suppose he did. But the thing is, heroin's been around for years, and there's always been junkies willing to kill someone to get a fix, and I really can't see how crack could be much *worse*. But you don't hear anything much about heroin these days. Just crack. Killer Crack. It's all just a big media hype.

But the thing about a media hype is it works. And I have to tell you, it has made me scared to death of crack addicts. And every time I read in the paper about some crack killing, the first thing I do is check the address and see if it's some neighborhood I've been in. And it usually is.

And the thing is, whether I've been there or not, I remember the address, and every time I get a new assignment I think back to what I read in the paper and try to figure out what I know of the area.

Now from what I remembered, Washington Heights is a big crack area. So is Harlem. 141st Street is on the border of both, and, as I recalled, the 140's were particularly bad. So I was apprehensive as I turned onto 141st Street: how bad is it going to be?

Pretty bad. And the further east I went, the worse it got. Half the buildings abandoned and boarded up. The other half looking like they ought to be.

I cruised by my building and checked it out. I do that sometimes when I'm particularly nervous, which is more often than I care to think about. About what I'd expected. A five story walkup in poor repair. Cracked concrete steps up to a closed wooden door. A glass transom overhead, and did I catch a sign of movement in it? I couldn't tell.

I went by and parked the car. Parking spaces abounded, which was good in that I could get one, and bad in that it indicated that no one in his right mind would want to park here.

I got out of my car, took my briefcase, and walked back to the building. There was no one hanging out on the front steps, but it was cold out, so there wouldn't be. I checked my notebook. Sherry Webber lived in apartment 51, which probably meant fifth floor, though in a building like this you couldn't be sure.

I looked up at the transom. Sure enough, there was movement behind it, and I could see the shadowy outline of what appeared to be someone's hat. Could it? No. You're imagining it. No one could be that tall. Well, come on, schmuck, you going in or not?

I walked up the steps, put my hand on the knob, and opened the door.

Jesus Christ! My worst nightmare. At least ten people hanging out in the grungy foyer. Ragged, strung-out, weird looking. I'm sure I projected some of it, but some of it I didn't. The guy with the hat, for instance, was tall enough to be seen through the transom. And some of the others, I know, had a glassy-eyed look that god never intended. They were all staring at me, and though none of them said anything, I could see their minds racing: "A honkey!" "A cop!" "What the fuck?" "Who the hell?" "Shit!"

My impulse was to turn and run, but I didn't. I'd like to have you think it was bravery, but it wasn't. It was fear. It was the feeling that gripped me at that moment that if I turned tail, if I *showed* fear, I was dead. So with all my adrenaline pumping like crazy, I stood my ground, and said real loud and aggressive, "Sherry Webber."

They stared at me as if I were from another planet, which was what I felt like.

"Sherry Webber," I demanded again. "She live here?"

There was a moment while they all kind of looked at each other, and then a girl somewhere in the back of the foyer said, "Upstairs."

I pointed a finger at her. "Thank you," I said. I pushed by the two guys next to the door and plunged up the stairs. It took an effort not to look back to see if anyone was following me.

At the top of the stairs there were two more guys hanging out on the 2nd floor landing.

"Sherry Webber," I yelled at them.

They gawked at me. I pushed by 'em, plunged up the next stairs.

Two more guys hanging out on the third floor. Shit. Didn't any of these people have apartments?

"Sherry Webber," I demanded.

One of them actually pointed up. I gave a curt nod of thanks and headed up, always putting more and more people between me and the safety outside.

No one on the next floor. Good. I couldn't take much more of this. At last I had time to look at the apartments. As expected, there were no numbers on the doors. Well, 51 should be 5th floor. One more flight.

Three people on the 5th floor landing. Two girls and a guy. Young. Teens, early twenties.

"Sherry Webber," I said again.

One of the girls pointed to the back of the hallway. I turned the corner, went there. There were two doors facing me. Numberless. I turned back.

"Which one."

"That one," she said.

I couldn't tell which one she was pointing to. I also thought I heard steps coming up the stairs.

"Which?" I said again, trying to keep the hysteria out of my voice.

She pointed again, and this time I could tell. The one to the left.

I turned and banged on it. Shit. Nothing. I banged again, louder this time. Christ, she made the appointment, wasn't she home?

And then, from deep within the apartment, came the faint voice. "Just a minute."

A minute, hell! I looked over my shoulder. They were all looking at me. And those *were* footsteps on the stairs.

"Who are you?" the guy said.

At that moment two other guys, both fairly young, appeared at the top of the stairs.

"I'm not here to bust her," I said. "I'm from her lawyer's office. I'm on her side."

"A lawyer," he said. "No shit. What the hell she need a lawyer?"

"She broke her leg. She's got money coming."

"Oh, yeah, money," he said.

Two more guys came up the stairs just in time to hear this. I didn't want them to think *I* had money for her.

"I mean we're going to get it for her," I said, stupidly. "From the insurance company."

He frowned. "She got insurance?"

"No, no," I said. My mind had given way, and I was about to explain the whole process of litigation to these guys, but at that moment the lock clicked back and the door opened. I whirled around in immense relief that immediately evaporated as I discovered the door had opened a mere two inches on a safety chain. From within came a maddeningly cheery sing-song, "Who is it?"

"Mr. Hastings from the lawyers office," I said. I was trying for crisp efficiency. The result was something akin to an hysterical shout.

The door slammed shut. My heart sank. Wrong apartment! It's not Sherry Webber, and she didn't call Rosenberg and Stone, and she isn't expecting me, and I'm stranded out here, and everyone's staring at me, and I'm about to do something slightly unprofessional like scream, or faint, or pee in my pants, and—the lock clicked back again and I suddenly realized she had just closed the door to take off the safety chain.

Standing in the doorway was a plump, sixtyish woman with a full-length cast.

"Sherry Webber?" I said.

She smiled. "Yes. You're the lawyer, aren't you?"

I didn't figure it was a good time to explain I was merely a private detective *employed* by the lawyer.

"Yes," I said, practically knocking her over in my haste to get into the apartment. I pushed by her, and then actually helped her close the door, just so I could make damn sure it was locked.

I followed her into the kitchen, and we sat down at the kitchen table. I opened my briefcase, took out a sign-up kit, and pulled out a fact sheet. As I took a pen out of my jacket pocket, I realized I was hyperventillating and having trouble breathing.

So did she. "You all right?" she said. "You out of breath?"

"That's a lotta stairs," I told her.

She nodded. "Yes. Lotta stairs. That's where I got hurt."

It was indeed. Sherry Webber's case was simple and straightforward. She'd been coming down the stairs from the 3rd to the 2nd floor, tripped on a cracked step, fallen, and broken her leg. I wrote down the facts of the case, had her sign hospital release forms to get her medical records, a request for the police report, and a retainer. The retainer, of course, was what it was all about. By signing it she authorized Richard Rosenberg to act as her attorney, and, in the event he received any money for her by way of a settlement, to retain one third of it as his fee.

The signup took about fifteen minutes. When it was done, I whipped out my Canon Snappy 50 and took pictures of her broken leg. The pictures were always the end of the signup. That's because, if the client doesn't sign the retainer, there's no reason to waste the film. So after I take the injury pictures, I'm done.

Except for the Location of Accident pictures. See, Richard has a rule that, if the accident occurred at the same location as the interview, I have to take the accident pictures as part of the signup. That's because Richard is cheap, and he doesn't want to pay me for taking the accident pictures as a separate assignment. So I had to take pictures of Sherry Webber's stairs.

I didn't want to do it. My Canon Snappy 50 is not the world's most expensive camera, but it retails for close to 100 bucks. I had a feeling if I whipped it out in front of the guys on the stairs it would look like half a gram of coke to them. Was I being paranoid? Damn right, but paranoid people get killed too. I would have liked to have taken Sherry Webber downstairs with me to point out where she fell, but with her in a hip-length cast that seemed unnecessarily cruel. And what the hell

kind of detective was I anyway, taking a sixty year old
woman with a broken leg along for protection? So I just
wished her well, gave her Richard's business card, and
went out to take the pictures myself.

I didn't take 'em. When I turned the corner of the 3rd
floor landing there were people on the stairs. Four of
'em. They were standing right in the spot where Sherry
Webber fell.

I hadn't seen these four on my way up the stairs. I
was sure of it. I'd have remembered 'em. The guys I'd
seen before had seemed scary to me, but these guys
were something else. It was as if, as soon as I'd got into
Sherry Webber's apartment, they had been rushed over
by Central Casting to play the part of junkies. They
were too good to be true. Motorcycle jackets. Army
coats. Chains. Headbands. Sideburns. Mustaches. Two-
day growths. Missing teeth. Scars. And, so help me god,
an eyepatch.

One of the guys was holding a glass pipe up for a
second guy, who was sucking on it. A third guy was
holding a cigarette lighter the size of a butane torch up
to the pipe. The fourth guy was just kind of drooling
and waiting his turn.

Holy shit! Crack addicts!

I looked at them. They looked at me. Shit. What was
I going to do? One thing I knew I was not going to do
was whip out my camera and start taking accident photos. Sorry, Richard, but I'm about to break one of your
rules. If I get out of here alive, I'll explain it to you.

I couldn't just stand there. And I wasn't going back
up. So I started down the stairs.

And one of them, the fourth guy who'd been waiting
his turn, said, "Hey, let the man through."

I wasn't sure whether he meant "man" as in "person," or "the Man" as in "cop," but I wasn't going to question him on it. I kept going.

And they parted for me, like the sea, the one guy even taking his mouth from the pipe.

I pushed through them, mumbling, "Sorry, guys," and pounded on down the stairs.

I took the last flight of steps rather fast. In fact it was an effort not to take 'em two at a time.

The lobby was still mobbed. I felt as if I were running a gauntlet. I weaved through the people to the front door and out.

I half ran, half walked to my car. I unlocked the door, got in, locked the door, switched off the code alarm, gunned the motor, and got the hell out of there. I wheeled around the corner, drove a block, took another corner, and headed west to the relative safety of Broadway.

I pulled into a meter, shut the car off, and sat there.

Holy shit! I thought the projects were dangerous. How bad is it going to be? Put a red star next to this one.

I sat there for about fifteen minutes, which was how long it took me to calm down. When I finally did, and I finally realized I was alive and out of there, and everything was all right, I began to think somewhat rationally and take stock of my situation.

As far as my job was concerned, unless something came in on the beeper, I was through for the day. I had no other assignments, except for taking Sherry Webber's accident pictures, and I'd made up my mind to tell Richard he could damn well have some other investigator who carried a gun go back and take those. So there I

was in Harlem with time on my hands and nothing to
do.

Except for Pamela Berringer.

Which is why, after thinking it over, I decided to call
on Darryl Jackson. I didn't know what I was going to
tell him. I had no plan or anything. But I realized no
matter how long I thought about it, I wasn't going to
come up with any plan. So what the hell, I might as
well sound him out. Maybe I'd learn something that
would *suggest* a plan. Maybe I wouldn't. At any rate, I
wouldn't be any worse off than I was now. Besides, the
time was right for it. I wasn't any too keen about calling
on some black pimp in Harlem, but then, after Sherry
Webber's place, how bad could it be?

I checked the address in my notebook. It was in the
West 120's. I pulled a U-turn on Broadway and headed
downtown.

The address was a brownstone a couple of blocks
east of Broadway. It wasn't a particularly inviting-
looking building, but the front door was propped open.
And there was no one in the foyer, which put it about
ten notches above Sherry Webber's place in my
estimation.

I parked my car and went up the front steps. No one
in the lobby, no one on the stairs. A row of mailboxes.
Darryl Jackson's name was there, listed as Apt. 4R. I
headed up the stairs.

I met no one. I reached the 4th floor and looked
around.

There were two apartments to a floor, one in the
front of the building and one in the back. Both doors
were at the top of the stairs. Neither door had a
number. The door to the front apartment was to the

right, the door to the back apartment was to the left. So, 4R could either mean 4th floor right or 4th floor rear. I'd been in a lot of buildings like this, and sometimes it meant one, and sometimes it meant the other. You flipped a coin.

There was music coming from the front apartment, so I chose right. I knocked on the door. There came the sound of steps, and then the door opened and a huge black man stared out at me.

"Yeah?" he demanded.

"Darryl Jackson?"

"Next door," he grunted, and jerked his thumb, giving me a look of disgust, as if *I* were the idiot who hadn't put the numbers on the doors.

To tell the truth, I was glad. This guy looked like he could have played fullback for the Jets, and trying to wrestle him out of a video tape would not have been my idea of a good time. Whatever Darryl Jackson was like would have to be an improvement.

I banged on the door to the left. No answer. I tried again. Nothing. Darryl Jackson wasn't home.

I was about to go when suddenly I realized this was my big chance. Darryl Jackson wasn't home. All I had to do was get into his apartment, find the tape, and that would be that. I'm sure that's what any private detective worth his salt would do in this situation.

Only, I couldn't do it. You see, I have this problem with locked doors. My problem is, I can't open them.

I stood there looking at the door. What was I going to do? Well, I knew a guy named Leroy Stanhope Williams who was one of Richard's clients and who also happened to be a professional thief, who could get in that door in nothing flat. But Leroy lived out in Queens, and even if he were home, by the time he got up here,

Darryl Jackson probably would have showed up and it would have been a hell of a mess. So what the hell was I going to do?

The answer I arrived at was: nothing. When I stopped to think about it, I realized burglarizing apartments was a little out of my line. If Darryl Jackson wasn't at home, I would just damn well come back some time when he was.

I knocked on the door one last time, just in case he'd been in the john or something, and hadn't heard me. As expected, there was no response. As an afterthought, I tried the doorknob. I turned it and pushed. And the door opened.

I couldn't believe it. What a schmuck. I stand in the hallway trying to figure out how to get the door open, and it's unlocked all the time. I went in and closed the door behind me.

The place was a wreck. The living room, at one time, had been nicely furnished, but you'd never know it now. Things were thrown everywhere. The cushions had been taken off the couch, slit open, and thrown about the room. Feathers covered everything. The couch itself had been tipped over, the bottom slit open, and the stuffing pulled out. Books had been knocked from the shelves and were strewn about the room. The rug had been pulled up and tossed in a crumpled pile in the corner.

Most everything had been smashed, but nothing seemed to have been stolen. A stereo system, that had occupied a cabinet had been pulled out and hurled on the floor. The cabinet itself had been pulled out from the wall and tipped over. The way I knew the stereo had been in the cabinet was that the plug still ran through it to an outlet in the wall.

A TV and VCR on a stand did not appear to have been touched, except that the VCR was the top-loading type, and the top had been popped open to reveal no tape inside.

In short, the apartment had not been burglarized, it had been searched. The thing was, I had no way of knowing if what the intruder had been looking for had been found.

That caught me up short. Intruder. The word was a double whammy. At the moment, *I* was the intruder. But there had been another intruder, the *real* intruder, and where was he now? Could I really be sure he had left?

Fear is relative. I'd felt fear in the crack house, and I felt fear now, and which was more intense? Who gives a shit? Intruder. What about the intruder? There was no noise before I knocked on the door, was there? I hadn't heard anything, except from the adjoining apartment. Didn't that mean no one was there? I wasn't sure. What if he'd heard my footsteps on the stairs, and kept quiet and hid? What if he was here now?

I looked around. On the far wall was a door to a hallway, and down it I could see two closed doors, presumably one to the bedroom and one to the bath. What if the guy was in there?

I have never had a worse moment of indecision. Every bone in my body was telling me to get the hell out of there, but there I was. A heaven sent opportunity. Something had happened here, and I didn't know what it was, did I, Mr. Jones? But it was going to make a hell of a difference to Pamela Berringer if I could find out. At the expense, of course, of scaring myself to death. I mean, shit, she's a fucking whore, for Christ's sake. I mean, I should get myself killed for a fucking whore?

Asshole, I told myself. Pompous, self-righteous asshole. Stand here and judge the woman not on her merits, but on the grounds that you're chicken-shit and you want an excuse to take the easy way out. Screw Pamela Berringer. What are *you* going to do?

I had to know. Scared as I was, I had to know. I didn't expect to find anything, but there was one thing I could learn: if the intruder had found what he was looking for. Cause if he'd found it, he would have stopped looking. So if there was anything in the apartment that wasn't torn up, it was a pretty good indication he'd found it. But if the whole place was wrecked, it was a pretty good indication he hadn't. And suppose, just suppose, he'd been looking for the tape.

I had to do it. I tiptoed across the room to the hallway. I reached the first door, put my hand on the knob, and flattened myself against the wall, as if I were a goddamn cop stalking a gunman. I don't know why I did it. *I* didn't have a gun, and if there was a killer in there, I was going to be dead no matter how I opened the door, but I did it just the same. I twisted the knob, and, with a jerk, slammed the door open.

Nothing. An empty bathroom. The door to the medicine cabinet was open, and the stuff inside had been strewn out on the floor, but otherwise it was a perfectly ordinary bathroom.

I tried the other door. Same technique. Flattened against the wall, turned and pushed.

The door flew open. I peered around the corner.

Nothing. The room had been ransacked, but there was no one in it. There was a closet, but the door was open, and as everything in it had been pulled out, there was nothing for anyone to be hiding behind.

The apartment was empty.

I heaved a huge sigh of relief. Great. I could make my inspection. See what I could learn.

My first glance told me the room had been totally wrecked, indicating the intruder had not found what he wanted. But I wanted to make sure.

I looked around. The dresser drawers had been pulled out and dumped on the floor. Ditto the drawers of a small desk unit. Both pieces of furniture had been tipped over.

The blankets and sheets had been pulled off the bed and tossed in a corner. The mattress had been slit open in all directions. Springs protruded through the holes. Cotton stuffing was everywhere. The mattress itself had been thrown back on the boxspring in a haphazard fashion, so it was resting diagonally, half on and half off the bed.

I walked around the corner of the bed and stopped short. There on the floor was a young black man in the sartorial splendor of a pimp. He was lying face down on the floor, half covered by the mattress. His head was turned to the side so I could see the profile of his face. His eye was open, glassy, staring, and there was a stream of saliva running down his chin.

He was dressed from head to toe in shocking pink, except for the one area where the pink gave way to a vivid red that seemed to be emanating from where the handle of the carving knife protruded from the middle of his back.

8

THE THING IS, I'd never found a dead body before. I
know this is a failing in a private detective. On TV, private detectives find 'em all the time. And they know
just what to do about it, too. They examine the body
and search the apartment for clues. Yeah, that's what a
TV detective would have done.

What I did was throw up.

I count it to my credit that I managed to get into the
bathroom before I did, but, having accomplished that
feat, I promptly heaved my cookies into the toilet.

If you think that's an extreme reaction, I don't. I said
this was the first time I'd ever found a dead body. It
was also the first time I'd ever *seen* one. Even the few
funerals I'd attended had always been closed-coffin.
This was my first dead man, period. And what a first.
Who would have thought the little pimp to have had so
much blood in him? The knife must have hit an artery
or vein or something, which ever the hell it is that
bleeds a lot. The blood had soaked through the pink
shirt, ran down his side, and formed a pool on the floor.
The wound was still seeping when I saw it, though I

didn't know enough about forensics to know what that indicated in terms of time of death, and, frankly, the thought didn't occur to me at the time. All that occurred to me was that I'd be better off in the bathroom, which turned out to be true, for even though I reacted promptly, I barely made it.

I sat on the floor in front of the toilet, feeling that hot flush you always feel in your face after you vomit. I took deep breaths, trying to calm down, and trying to get my thoughts together.

What should I do? I knew what I was supposed to do. I was supposed to call the police, but should I do it? I didn't know. If I called the police, I'd have to explain why I was there. I'd have to tell 'em about Pamela Berringer. Somehow, in my code of ethics that didn't seem right.

What if I didn't call the police? What if I beat it the hell out of there, pretended it didn't happen, and let someone else discover the body? Not good. Forget the fact that it might be ages before anyone else came here, which would make a huge difference in whether the medical examiner could pinpoint the time of death. Consider the fact that that would make me an accessory to murder. Could they prove it? They sure as shit could. I'd left fingerprints all over the apartment. In my present state I couldn't even remember everything I'd touched. Unless I wanted to do a thorough housecleaning, my fingerprints would be there. And if I did clean up, I'd probably eliminate the murderer's fingerprints as well. Another count of accessory after that fact. Screw that. What about the fingerprints? Could they ever find me to match 'em up? No. Shit, yes. The videotape. They find the videotape and get a lead to Pamela Berringer. She talks and implicates me. Then they take my fingerprints. No. You're just being paranoid. Maybe they talk to you, but they don't really consider you a suspect and—Shit. The guy next door. The potential Jet fullback. He tells the police about the guy who knocked on the door of the wrong apartment. The police let him take a look at me and that's that. I was trying to get into Darryl Jackson's apartment. So they take my fingerprints to see if I did. I've already lied to them about it, so, instead of being a witness, I'm the number one suspect.

That thought tipped the scale. Sorry, Pamela. I'll protect you if I can. But I'm no hero. I'm Stanley Hastings, bloody fucking coward, and I haven't got the stomach for it, as you can see. I gotta call the cops.

You have to understand what happened next, because it's going to sound stupid to you. I know because it sounds stupid to me now, thinking about it, but it didn't at the time.

Having made the decision to call the cops, I got up from the bathroom floor and was not at all surprised to find I was shaky on my feet. I grabbed a hold of the sink to steady myself, leaving a few more fingerprints, but what did that matter now, since I was calling the cops anyway. I closed the mirror on the medicine cabinet and looked at myself. I looked like shit. I splashed some cold water on my face and rinsed out my mouth, which made me feel a little better. Then I flushed the toilet.

It didn't flush. It was one of those old fashioned types with a tank up on the wall and a pull chain, but when I pulled the chain nothing happened. Either the stopcock was stuck or the tank was empty. At any rate it didn't work.

And that's when I did the thing that doesn't make any sense—the thing I have to explain. See, I knew I was gonna call the cops, and I didn't want 'em to come in and see I puked in the toilet. And what makes it stupid is, I'm not macho, and I don't pretend to be. And if the cops asked me what I did when I found the body, I'd tell 'em the first thing I did was throw up. But to me there was a difference between telling 'em that, and having a whole bunch of homicide dicks roaming around the apartment saying to each other, "Hey, look here where this guy blew his lunch in the toilet." I didn't want that. Somehow it made a difference.

Which is why I went out of my way to flush the toilet. I closed the toilet seat, stood on it, reached up, and slid the cover off the tank. I reached my hand in to find the toggle and jiggle it. And my hand felt something strange. It wasn't water and it wasn't metal. It was plastic. I grabbed it and pulled it out.

It was a heavy white plastic bag, tied shut with a twist-tie. My father-in-law manufactured bags just like it, in fact, he might have even made this one. Whatever was in it was pretty large, which was why it had been displacing so much water in the tank, and why the toilet wouldn't flush.

I hopped down from the toilet, sat on the seat, and opened the bag. Inside were six VHS video cassettes.

Which made it a brand new ballgame.

Here it was, the evidence the murderer had been looking for. The thing the murderer had killed for. He hadn't found it, though someone who could overlook such an obvious hiding place would have to be almost as big an asshole as I am. He hadn't found it, but I had. By the modern investigative technique, detectus vomitus. What a guy.

So what now? What the hell did I do now? I'd painted myself into a corner. By my own reasoning, I had to call the police, but what then? I couldn't give 'em the tapes. Pamela Berringer was undoubtedly on one, if not all of 'em. I couldn't do that to her. Even if she killed him, I couldn't do that to her.

That thought caught me up short. Christ. Did I mean that? Even if she killed him. I mean, whoa, back up. A few minutes ago you were having problems about helping a hooker, and now you're just casually saying you'd help a murderer? Where's your moral perspective? Where's your values? You have trouble rationalizing her being a hooker, but no trouble rationalizing her killing her pimp?

Asshole! Cut it out. This guy was not killed to test your moral integrity. Think. What the hell are you going to do?

I didn't know. I knew I had to call the cops, and I knew I couldn't give 'em the tapes, and I knew I couldn't give 'em Pamela Berringer. But I didn't know how to do it.

I tried to think what a *real* private detective would do in this case. I immediately dismissed the thought. Screw that. That's the mistake I always make. A real private detective wouldn't *be* in this case, and if he were, his biggest concern would be making a fee. Never mind a real detective. What would a *TV* detective do in this case?

Well, one thing for sure—he wouldn't sit here like an

asshole trying to figure out what to do until the cops swooped down and grabbed him. A TV detective wouldn't let the cops get a hold of those tapes, and dammit, neither would I.

I got up, pulled the chain, and flushed the toilet. It worked fine now, without the bag of videotapes clogging things up. I climbed up on the toilet seat again, and slid the cover back on the tank. I hopped down, pulled off a few yards of toilet paper, and wadded it up. I hopped back up and polished the sides and top of the toilet tank. I was going to leave fingerprints in the apartment all right, there was no way for that, but I didn't have to leave 'em where they'd start the cops thinking in the right direction.

I grabbed the bag and got out of there. There was no one in the hall, no one on the stairs. I got in my car and drove off.

I cruised the side streets about ten blocks away from the apartment, looking for a place to ditch the tapes. I couldn't be too picky. Minutes were precious. I had to go back, and I not only had to get back before anyone found the body, I had to get back quick enough to be able to pretend I'd only been there once. That was an iffy proposition, if the football player had any idea what time it was when I'd knocked on *his* door. I realized *I* didn't know exactly when that was. It seemed an eternity, but probably couldn't have been more than fifteen minutes ago. Which was still too long. When you find a body, you don't sit around for half an hour hoping the guy will wake up, you call the police.

I drove by a dumpster, the large type they have by construction sites. I stopped the car, got out, and took a look. Pretty good. It was bout half full, so, on the one hand, it wouldn't be dumped for a while, but, on the other, there was enough stuff in it so the bag wouldn't stand out.

I looked up and down the street. No one was in sight. I reached in and slid the bag of videotapes down the side of the dumpster. I leaned over and pushed it right near the bottom. Then I pulled a bag of garbage over it.

I stood up and looked around. No one had seen me. O.K. Not great, but the best I could do.

I got in the car and pulled out. All right, now to beat it back there and call the cops. And tell 'em what? Shit. I still didn't know. I wasn't going to tell 'em the real reason. I wasn't going to tell 'em about Pamela. But I had to tell 'em something. You didn't just go calling on pimps for no reason. So why was I there?

A phone booth on the corner brought me to my senses. I slammed on the brakes, hit a patch of ice, fish-tailed, spun the wheel desperately, pulled out of it, swerved to the side of the street, and stopped. I hopped out of the car and ran to the phone.

I fished a quarter out of my pocket, dropped it in, pulled out my notebook, found the number, and punched it in. Miracle. The phone worked. It rang. Once. Twice. Three times. Oh shit, be home.

He was. On the fourth ring the phone was picked up, and I heard the cultured, resonant tones of Leroy Stanhope Williams.

"Hello?"

"Leroy. Stanley Hastings."

"Ah, Stanley. It's been a while. How good of you to call."

"Look, Leroy, I'm in a jam. I need your help."

"What did you do? Lock yourself out of your car?"

"No. It's serious. Seconds count. You got a pencil?"

"No."

"Get one."

There was a second's pause, then I heard the sound of the receiver being put down. I'd never talked to Leroy quite like that, and it must have taken him a moment to realize I wouldn't have if it hadn't been really important.

He was back in seconds, crisp and efficient.

"O.K. I got one."

"Good. Take this down."

I read him Darryl Jackson's address and phone number out of my notebook.

"You got that?" I asked.

"Yes."

"Read it back to me."

He did.

"O.K. Call Rosenberg and Stone right away. Tell 'em your name's Darryl Jackson, you broke your leg, you're home now, and you want someone to come right over."

"Fine. Anything else?"

"Yeah. You better do it from a pay phone. I wouldn't want the call traced back to you."

"It's that serious?"

"Yeah. It's that serious," I said. Then, partly to make up for being so brusque, and partly because it mattered, I added. "One more thing."

"Yes?"

"This Darryl Jackson happens to be a pimp, so it might be better if you didn't sound as if you'd just stepped out of the Royal Shakespeare Company production of Othello."

Leroy laughed. "Don' you fret. Ah gib it mah best jibe."

Leroy's best jive was none too good, but under the circumstances it would pass. I hung up the phone, breaking the connection, then picked it up again and pretended I was making a call. I couldn't take a chance on any long-winded person acing me out of the phone. I hung onto it and waited.

It was the longest wait of my life. Jesus Christ, what's taking 'em so long. The fucking incompetents. Richard ought to fire the lot of 'em. Then I started getting worried. What if it isn't me? What if they give it to some other investigator? Bullshit. I'm in Harlem. They know that. Why would they give it to some one working Brooklyn or Queens when I'm right there. Unfortunately, I had an answer. Because they're stupid. Because they're two of the most lame-brained girls I've ever met, and how can I count on them to even check the assignment book and see I'm in Harlem. It would be just like them to—

My beeper went off. Its high-pitched beep, beep, beep never sounded so good. I shut it off, hung up, picked up the phone again, dropped my quarter, and punched in Richard's number before the second, back-up beep even went off. The phone was already ringing when I shut that off.

Wendy/Cheryl answered the phone. "Rosenberg and Stone."

"Agent 005."

"Well, that was fast."

"I believe in service. What's up?"

As I said it, I thought, shit, this won't be it, she's so stupid she's gonna send me out to Brooklyn for something else.

But she didn't. This was it. A Darryl Jackson had broken his leg, and—

I stopped listening. I didn't have to. I already had his name and address written in my notebook, just like it should be, so I didn't have to write it again. But now it was accounted for.

I waited till she was finished, told her I'd take it, and hung up.

I hopped in my car, sped back to Darryl Jackson's apartment building, parked the car, grabbed my brief-case, and got out.

I took the stairs two at a time. Again, I saw no one.

I went into Darryl Jackson's apartment and closed the door behind me. I took a quick look in the bedroom, just to be sure the body was still there, though why it shouldn't have been is beyond me.

I went back in the living room and picked up the phone. I could have dialed 911, but I guess I'm just a romantic at heart, because, even in the midst of the predicament I was in, I couldn't resist dialing "0" instead, so that when the operator answered, I could say the words I'd been reading in detective stories all my life, ever since I was a small boy: "Operator, get me the police."

9

THE FIRST COPS through the door were uniform cops. Two of 'em, one tall and one short. They must have been cruising the neighborhood when the call came over the radio.

They came in with their guns drawn. They'd heard it was a homicide and they weren't taking any chances.

They seemed surprised to see me, though I didn't know why. I mean, dead bodies don't report themselves—*someone* has to phone 'em in.

The short cop seemed to be in charge. "Who the hell are you?" he demanded.

I'm easily intimidated, and of the things that intimidate me, guns and cops are high up on the list. And my nerves were not in great shape at the time, having first discovered a dead body, and second decided to lie my way out of it. So I count it to my credit that I didn't break down and confess then and there.

"I found the body. I called the police."

That didn't really answer his question, but it seemed to be the response he was looking for.

"Where is it?"

I pointed to the bedroom. "In there."

He nodded to the tall cop. "Stay with him."

Short cop went into the bedroom. Tall cop moved over to stand next to me. He hadn't said a word yet, and he didn't now. But he still had his gun out, and to me that spoke volumes.

Short cop returned from the bedroom. "It's a homicide all right."

Tall cop finally spoke. "So what do we do?"

"Nothing. We hold him here until the homicide boys get here. Until they do, we don't touch anything." He turned to me. "You touch anything?"

"Sure," I said.

His head jerked up. "What?" he said ominously.

"I said, yes, I did."

He glared at me. "You're not supposed to touch anything in a homicide."

"I didn't know it was a homicide until I found the body."

He thought that over. "What did you touch?"

"I don't know. I can't remember everything. I know I touched the phone."

"Why?"

"To call you."

"Oh."

"And I touched the toilet."

"The toilet?"

"Yeah."

"Why'd you touch the toilet?"

"I touched it when I threw up."

"Oh." He gave me a contemptuous look. After all, he'd just seen the body and *he* hadn't thrown up.

Footsteps pounded up the stairs and three more men came in. They were in plain clothes. The boys from homicide.

It's hard to tell a cop's rank when they're in plain clothes, but the last one through the door appeared to be in charge. He was older, bigger, beefier, and he had that look of authority about him.

At any rate, he *took* charge.

"Where is it?" he snapped at the uniform cops.

"In there," said short cop.

"Check it out."

The two younger homicide cops went into the bedroom.

"Who's this guy?" he asked, jerking his thumb over his shoulder in my direction.

"He found the body and phoned it in."

He grunted and turned to me and my heart sank. Shit! Of all the unlucky breaks. I *knew* him. The first and only time I'd met him he'd been in uniform, so I knew he was a sergeant. He looked different in plain clothes, but it was him all right. He was the guy who'd interrogated me when I brought in a bullet in the Albrect case. I'd been lucky enough to get out of it that time, but it would take more than luck for me to get out of it now.

I hoped to god he wouldn't recognize me. There was no reason that he should. I knew him, but then he was the only sergeant who'd ever interrogated me. He must have interrogated thousands of guys in his time, so why should he remember me.

Then it hit me. Schmuck. You're a private detective, and that's why you're here. And the minute you tell him he'll know.

"Who the hell are you?" he demanded. He was looking at me kind of funny, like he couldn't quite place me.

"Stanley Hastings. I found the body."

"Oh yeah? And how'd you happen to do that?"

"I had an appointment to see him. When I got here he was dead."

"How'd you get in?"

"The door was open."

"Standing open?"

"No. Just unlocked."

"Is it your habit just to walk into people's apartments?"

"I knocked on the door. There was no answer, so I tried the knob."

"Why? What if he just wasn't home?"

"He had to be home. He'd just called for an appointment."

"What do you mean, an appointment? What do you do?"

This was it. "I'm a private detective."

"What?!"

His eyes blinked, and I could see it starting to dawn on him.

"Wait a minute. What kind of private detective?"

"I work for the law firm of Rosenberg and Stone. This guy called them, said it was an accident case and he wanted an investigator to come over. They beeped me and sent me here."

He blinked again. "Ambulance chaser," he muttered. He frowned, then his eyes widened. "Son of a bitch!" he said.

There was no mistaking the look in his eyes. He knew me. He knew me, and I was sunk.

He whirled around. "Daniels!" he bellowed.

One of the plain clothes cops stuck his head out of the bedroom.

"Sir?"

"Take this guy downtown and hold him as a material witness. Get a signed statement out of him. And don't let him leave till I get there."

Daniels came over and put his hand on my arm. "O.K., buddy, let's go."

I didn't like his hand on my arm, but there were a lot of things about the situation I didn't like, and I figured I was in enough trouble without making any more, so I let it go.

"That's my briefcase," I said, pointing to where I'd left it on the floor.

"We'll take care of it," the Sergeant said. He jerked his head toward the door, and Daniels ushered me out.

He let me go down the stairs under my own power, probably my reward for not resisting the hand on my arm. I had a feeling if I'd tried to pull away, he'd have yanked me down every flight.

His car was parked right out front. Black, unmarked. He leaned me against it and patted me down for a weapon, probably not wanting to be shot in the back of the head on the way to the precinct. I didn't appreciate the search, but I understood the sentiment. He put me in the back seat, which was what I'd expected, particularly after the frisking. He got in and chauffeured me downtown. The whole time he didn't say a word, again, what I'd expected.

At the precinct he took me upstairs to a small interrogation room, called in a stenographer, and took my statement.

It was my first time being interrogated as a murder suspect, and if I hadn't been in so much trouble, I might have found it interesting. What was interesting about it was how dull it actually was. See, part of the interrogation technique seems to be to ask the same questions over and over with slight variations, in the hope of catching the suspect in a contradiction. At least that was Daniels' technique. He seemed a nice enough guy, as cops go, though perhaps a little too young and a little too serious.

First he just let me talk. When I was finished, he asked questions. Like the sergeant, he immediately pounced on the one weak point in my story.

"You say the door was unlocked?"

"Yes."

"But it was closed?"

"That's right."

"Completely closed?"

"What do you mean, completely closed? That's like a little bit pregnant. It was closed. Closed is closed."

"I mean it wasn't ajar. Even the slightest. If you pushed against it, it wouldn't open."

"That's right."

"Then you *did* push on it?"

"I knocked on it. I suppose I pushed on it."

"If you hadn't, how would you know it was completely closed?"

"That's right. I must have pushed on it."

"But it didn't open when you pushed on it?"

"That's right."

"And that's because it was completely closed. Even though it wasn't locked, the catch was in place, holding the door from opening."

"The catch?"

"The mechanism. The thing connected to the door-knob that holds the door shut. I don't know what you call it."

"I don't either."

"All right, but you know what I mean. The mechanism was engaged, so the door would not open just by pushing on it. It would only open if you turned the knob."

"That's right."

"And you *did* turn the knob?"

"Yes."

"Why?"

"To get in."

"That's not an answer. The question is why did you do it?"

"To get in. To see the guy."

He frowned. Rubbed his chin. "Let me be very specific about this. I'm telling you you're not answering the question. I know you turned the knob to get in and see the guy. What I'm asking for is an explanation. I'll spell it out for you. It is not normal behavior for people to let themselves into strangers' apartments. I want to know why you did so in this case."

"Look. I'd been banging on the door and got no answer. I thought the guy might be in the bathroom or something and didn't hear me, so I kept trying. I still got no answer."

"So?"

"So, the guy had to be there. I'd just talked to my office. They said the guy had just called and was there now waiting for me. He *had* to be there."

"But he wasn't."

"No."

"So you tried to get into the apartment."

"No. I didn't."

"I thought you said you did."

"No. I said I opened the door."

"Right. And would you please answer the question we keep coming back to: *why* did you open the door? Particularly as you now claim you weren't trying to get into the apartment?"

"The guy had a bad leg. At least, that's what they told me. For all I knew he was laid up in bed and couldn't get to the door. And that's why he couldn't hear me. Or why I couldn't hear him. That's why I wanted to open the door. Not to get into the apartment. To call out and see if anybody was there."

He was looking at me very skeptically now. "You say you had no intention of entering the apartment?"

"That's right."

"Then why did you?"

"I opened the door and looked in. The apartment was a wreck. Obviously something had happened."

"And what did you think had happened?"

"I don't know."

"But you went in?"

"Yes. Wouldn't you?"

"Yes. But I'm a cop. That's my job. Why did *you* go in?"

"To see if the guy was all right."

"What made you think he might not be all right?"

"Apartments don't wreck themselves."

"They certainly don't."

"And the guy wasn't answering the door."

"So you suspected foul play?"

Despite myself, I smiled.

He frowned. "What's so funny?"

"I'm sorry. I just can't believe you really use those words."

"What?"

"Next you're going to ask me if I thought there was a perpetrator."

His face flushed. "Now look here—" he began. He caught himself up short, probably remembering the presence of the stenographer. "All right. Could you please answer the question?"

"Did I suspect foul play? Yes, I did. I figured someone had been there and wrecked the apartment, and might have done harm to Mr. Jackson. That's why I went in."

"So you thought someone had been in the apartment?"

"That's right."

"I mean an intruder?"

"Yes."

"And it would have had to have been very recent, right? I mean, you knew that, because Darryl Jackson had just called your office."

"That's right."

"So the intruder might have still been there."

"Maybe, but I didn't think so. I'd been banging on the door for some time. And, of course, I'd been listening for any sounds from the apartment. And I hadn't heard anything. So I figured he'd gone."

"But you didn't know that?"

"I couldn't be sure."

"The guy might have still been there?"

"It's possible."

"But you went in?"

"Yes."

"Do you carry a gun?"

"You know I don't. You frisked me, didn't you?"

"This is for the record. Do you carry a gun?"

"No. I don't."

"Didn't that make you a little nervous, going into that apartment without a gun?"

"Yes."

"Well?"

"Well, what?"

"Why did you do it?"

"I told you. To see if the guy was all right."

"Weren't you scared?"

"Sure I was scared." I shook my head, held up my hand. "Look. Let me tell you something. About this job of mine. The clients I go see, for the most part, are not particularly wealthy. I have to go into some pretty undesirable neighborhoods. The truth is, I'm scared most of the time. But I have to do it. It's my job. Now I'll tell you. When I got that door open and saw what had happened, I was scared to death. I didn't want to go in there. But I felt I had to do it. So I did it. And that's all there is to it."

He sat there looking at me for a few moments. "All right. Let me see if I understand this correctly. You work for this law firm, this Rosen-something—"

"That's right. Rosenberg and Stone."

"They advertise on TV. People call in and ask to see an investigator. The office beeps you and sends you out. Is that right?"

"That's right."

"In this case, you were told to go to this address, the

guy was there waiting for you. You went up, knocked on the door and got no answer."

"That's right."

"So you did everything you could to get into the apartment."

"I wouldn't say I did everything I could. I knocked on the door. I tried the knob."

"Why?"

"What do you mean, why? We've been all over this."

"Yes, we've been all over this, but we haven't gotten an answer. Not one that makes sense. I mean, you seem to be an incredibly dedicated employee. I mean, if the guy wasn't home, big deal. No skin off your nose. It's not your fault. You just report to the office the guy wasn't there, and you come back some time when he *is* there."

I shrugged. "Yeah."

"Well, isn't that right?"

"I suppose so."

"Well, why not?"

I looked down at the table. Sighed. Then, very reluctantly, said, "All right. Look. You gotta understand the way I work." I looked up at him. "I don't get paid for an eight-hour day."

He looked at me. "What's that got to do with it?"

"I only get paid when I'm on a case."

"So what?"

"When I turn in my paysheets, I can't just say I was working. Every hour I charge for has to be attributed to a particular case."

"So?"

"Well, my boss is cheap. He won't pay me for work in progress. He only pays me when a case is done."

He looked at me ironically. "Gee, that's tough. What's the point?"

"Well, this guy, Darryl Jackson. If he's home, I talk to him, I sign him up, I put in two hours on my paysheet, and I get paid. If he's not home, I don't get two hours, I get one hour, the hour I spent getting there. And I don't put it on my paysheet. I put it on a separate paysheet marked "pend," and it sits in my briefcase until I finally get to see the guy. Since I get paid bi-weekly, if I miss this week's paysheet, it'll be close to three weeks before I can turn it in. One way it's two hours on my paysheet, and the other it's one hour in my briefcase, and I need all the hours I can get."

He looked at me contemptuously. "So that's what the guy meant to you? Two hours on your paysheet?"

I shrugged. "Aw hey, come on."

I looked down at the table and tried to look a bit sheepish, but inside I was jumping up and down. Holy shit. I did it. Home free. I was sure of it. Daniels had been skeptical at first, but now he was sold. Self-interest is always an acceptable motivation. It's universal. Show a little greed, and anyone will buy it.

And I'd played it right, too. If I'd sprung it on him at the start, he'd have been skeptical. But by making him drag it out of me, I'd sold him on it. Hell, he'd sold himself. The way I figured it, it was over.

It was too. Daniels turned to the stenographer. "O.K. Type it up and have him sign it."

"Then I'm free to go?"

"I'm afraid not. We'll have to check this out, of course. And the Sergeant wants to see you. In the meantime, we'd like to take your fingerprints."

Jesus Christ. Just when I thought I'd got away with it. "My fingerprints? What, are you booking me?"

"Certainly not," he said, I thought, somewhat suavely. "But you touched things in that apartment. We're taking fingerprints up there, of course, and we're gonna need to know which ones are yours."

I couldn't argue with that. It was also quite a relief. I told him I'd be happy to cooperate.

He muttered something that sounded like thanks, and left.

A few minutes later a uniform cop came in and took me off to be fingerprinted. He took me down to a large room on the main floor that was filled with cops and various other people, whom I assumed were suspects, seeing as how a number of them were being finger-printed and booked. I waited my turn and was finger-printed too. Of course, I wasn't being booked, and any resemblance between me and a common criminal was entirely coincidental and not to be inferred. Still, I was glad I didn't see anyone there I knew, as I doubt if they'd have been able to tell the difference.

There was a difference, however, and the difference was, while they took my fingerprints, they didn't take my picture, as they did with everybody else I saw being fingerprinted. So, officially, I was not being booked. I was glad. Being booked for murder would have kind of put a damper on my day.

When I was finished, the cop took me back upstairs to the interrogation room and left me to my own devices. My first device was to look out the door after him. I discovered that he had stationed himself right outside in the hall, just in case there was any misunderstanding on my part about their desire to have me stick around.

I went back, sat down, and took stock of the situation. All in all, things didn't look that bad. I'd gotten through the interrogation with flying colors. I'd sold

Daniels on my story. Hell, I'd even gotten in that zinger
about the perpetrator. That may not seem like much to
you, but for me that was cocky as hell. At any rate,
things were working out. So far, so good. I was over the
first hurdle.

The second would be the Sergeant, and I wasn't
really looking forward to that. He had recognized me—
I was sure of it—and that was bound to make him suspicious as hell. But when I thought about it, I realized
there wasn't much he could do about it. O.K., so I'd
brought in a bullet once, which made me involved in
two murder cases, which, of course, was suspicious. But
that was it. In this case, I'd covered myself so well,
there was really nothing he could do. He'd check with
Rosenberg and Stone, and my story would check out.
Of course, if I'd just called Wendy/Cheryl and told her
to cover for me, I'd have been in trouble—they'd have
broken her in thirty seconds. But I hadn't done that.
Thanks to Leroy, I was totally safe. The Sergeant could
question Wendy/Cheryl till he was blue in the face, and
she couldn't blow it for me, because there was nothing
to blow. As far as she knew it was all true.

I was feeling cocky enough by the time Daniels got
back with my statement to give him a little grief.

"Hey," I said. "How long do I have to stick around?"

"I told you. The Sergeant wants to see you. And we
have to check your statement."

"Yeah, well you should have checked it out by now. I
wanna go home."

He shrugged. "Sorry."

"Look, if you're not charging me, you got no right to
hold me."

"This is true."

"Well, are you charging me?"

He shrugged. "Not at the present time."

I didn't like that, and he knew I didn't like that, and he knew I knew that was why he said it, and I liked that even less. "You're telling me you're not charging me, but you're not going to let me leave?"

He shrugged again, which I was beginning to find an annoying habit. "I'm just telling you to stick around, that's all. I'm sure you don't want to force the issue."

That sounded like a threat. It was also true. I'm a big coward, and forcing issues is not one of my strong suits. Still, I didn't like being pushed around. "All right," I said. "But whether you're charging me or not, I'd like to call my lawyer."

He thought that over. "I would certainly never stand in the way of a person trying to contact his attorney," he said.

"God bless Miranda," I said.

He led me down the hall to a pay phone, and withdrew to a discreet distance. I dropped in a quarter and called Rosenberg and Stone.

Wendy/Cheryl seemed more flustered that usual when she answered the phone. She also seemed surprised to hear from me. She put me on hold, however, and seconds later Richard's high-pitched nasal twang filtered through the wire.

"Hello?"

"Richard, Stanley. Look, I'm—"

"You're at the police station?"

"Yes. They're holding me without a charge, and—"

"I know all about it. The police are here now. You say they haven't charged you?"

"No, but—"

"Fine. Just sit tight. I'm sure everything will be all right."

The phone clicked dead.

I hung up. As I did so, Daniels was right at my elbow, guiding me back into the room. I needed guidance. My head was spinning. This wasn't like Richard. Richard thrived on confrontations and loved bopping cops around. By rights he should have been ranting and raving and storming the police station demanding my release and raising merry hell.

Before I had any time to think about it the door opened and the Sergeant himself came in, accompanied by the stenographer, who went and took up his position at the end of the table. The Sergeant was holding some papers which I assumed was my signed statement. He turned to me.

"Mr. Hastings?" he said.

"Yes."

"I'm Sergeant McAullif, homicide. I'm in charge of this investigation. I've been going over your signed statement, and I'd just like to ask you a few questions."

"Of course," I said.

Something was wrong. I mean aside from the obvious fact that I'd found a dead body and was mixed up in a murder investigation, something was very wrong. Because the Sergeant knew me, I was sure of it, and yet he wasn't letting on. He wasn't jumping down my throat, saying, "You again!" He was being polite and crisp and efficient, and treating the whole thing as just routine. And that just wasn't right.

I had no time to think about it before the questions started coming, and then, of course, I had to concentrate on them.

And I knew the first question he was going to ask me. He was going to ask me about the door.

He didn't.

"Now, then, Mr. Hastings. I just want to get this straight. You work for the law firm of Rosenberg and Stone. They beeped you, you called in, and they told you you had an appointment to go see a client. They gave you Darryl Jackson's name and address and you copied it into your notebook, is that right?"

"Yes."

"Could I see your notebook, please?"

I took it out and handed it to him. He opened it and turned to the page.

"Ah, yes. Here it is. Darryl Jackson, 307 West 127th Street, Apartment 4R. And the phone number. I see this is the last entry in your notebook."

"Of course. It's my last assignment. I just got it."

"Now, the entry just above it: Sherry Webber, 150 West 141st Street. What is that?"

"That's the client I called on before I called on Darryl Jackson. I'd just finished that assignment when they beeped me. That's why I got the Darryl Jackson case. I was in Harlem already."

He nodded. "That makes sense. Now, I notice you first wrote 105 West 141st Street, then crossed it off and changed it to 150."

"That's right."

"Why."

"I had the address wrong. So I checked the address and changed it."

"How'd you check it?"

"I called Sherry Webber."

"And then you went there?"

"Absolutely. You can check the signed retainers in my briefcase. Or call Sherry Webber. She won't remember my name, but she'll verify I was there."

"And the time you left?"

Ah, so that was it. I'd been trying to figure out what the hell he was getting at, and it had been making me a little nervous that I couldn't. But this was it. The time element.

"I'm not sure she'll know the exact time I left. But my appointment was originally for between 11:00 and 12:00, and I had to drop off some pictures, so when I called her I pushed it back to between 12:00 and 1:00. I'm sure she'll remember that."

"What time did you actually get to her apartment?"

"About 12:30."

"And when did you leave?"

"I'm not sure. A little after 1:00."

"And when were you beeped? While you were still at Sherry Webber's?"

"No. I'd left. I was driving home and my beeper went off."

"So you stopped the car and called in?"

"Yes."

He pulled a notebook out of his jacket pocket and referred to it. "And you talked to a Miss Wendy Millington?"

"I talked to one of the secretaries at Rosenberg and Stone. Frankly, I can't tell 'em apart on the phone."

"And Miss Millington gave you Darryl Jackson's name and address. You copied it into your notebook, went to that address, banged on the door, got no answer, found the door unlocked, walked in, and found the body?"

"That's right."

The Sergeant sighed and shook his head. "That's the problem."

I automatically tensed. "What is?"

"We checked with Wendy Millington, of course. And she confirms your story. A Darryl Jackson called in, asked for an appointment, she beeped you, gave you the name and address, and sent you right over. We checked the assignment log, and sure enough, she wrote down that Agent 005, which we have confirmed is you, was assigned to be at Darryl Jackson's apartment between the hours of 1:00 and 2:00."

"So?"

The Sergeant shrugged, and I realized where Daniels had got it from. "The only thing is, Wendy Millington had Darryl Jackson's address listed as 309 West 127th Street." He smiled, but his eyes bored into mine. "Now, would you mind telling me how it happens that you had Darryl Jackson's address *right*, when Wendy Millington gave it to you, and she had it *wrong*?

10

IN THE COURSE of my less than illustrious career as an actor/writer, I have been many things and held many jobs. And in all the positions in which I have found myself, one thing has proved to be universally true: no matter how promising any job, or situation, or opportunity might seem to be, eventually it would come to naught. The school I was teaching at would fold, the company I was working for would go union and I would not be allowed to join, the magazine editor who had seemed so happy with my article would publish someone else's instead. And I would be fucked.

This happened to me so regularly and so invariably, that I soon came to expect to be fucked, and when I was fucked, it was never any surprise to me, but merely an inevitable outcome that I had been anticipating and wondering just when it was going to occur. And it happened so often that after a while I never just thought of myself as being fucked, but always automatically referred to the *degree* to which I was fucked, as in, slightly fucked, or, very fucked, or, a little bit fucked.

Using this as a yardstick, it was possible to access my current situation.

I was totally fucked.

I tried not to let it show. After all, if I let it show, the game would have been up. Then, I suppose, totally fucked would have moved into the realm of permanently and irrevocably fucked. I kept my face composed, and fought for time.

"She what?" I said.

"She got it wrong. She had the wrong address. It's in the book. The assignment log. We went down there. We verified it. She wrote it down wrong. Now can you please tell me how you had the right address, when she gave it to you and she had it wrong?"

"I don't know. I can't understand it." I pretended to think about it, which was easy, as what I was doing was thinking about it. Then it came to me. "Unless. . . ."

"Unless? Unless what?"

"Well," I said. "I'm not that familiar with how the office works, but I think it's like this. A call comes in. The girl writes down the information on a piece of paper, all right? Then if it becomes an assignment, she beeps me, she gives me the assignment, and then she copies it into the assignment log."

"So?"

"So that's what happened. The call came in. She wrote down the address right on the sheet of paper. She gave it to me right, and then she copied it into the book wrong. See?"

He shrugged. "That sounds very logical."

"Oh?"

"Yeah. In fact, I spoke to your boss, this Mr. Rosenberg and that's exactly what he said. He said the same thing. I spoke to Wendy Millington. She said the same thing too."

"There you are," I said.

He shrugged again. "Well, yes and no."

"What do you mean by that?"

"She couldn't find the paper."

"The paper?"

"Yes. The paper. The paper she wrote the address down on before she transferred it into the log. Naturally, we wanted to look at the paper. She didn't have it."

"No?"

"No. She had every other paper from every other case that came in today, but not that one. You see?"

"Yeah. She lost it. I'm not surprised."

"Funny she would have lost that one piece of paper."

I shook my head. "Not with my luck."

"Obviously, we need that piece of paper to corroborate your story. It wasn't on Wendy Millington's desk. It wasn't in her wastebasket. The other girl, ah, Miss Cheryl Reeves, didn't have it either." He paused, looked at me. I said nothing. "We mean to find that paper. When it turned out the two girls didn't have it, your boss, Rosenberg, started getting crusty, wanted to know if we had a warrant. Of course we didn't."

He stopped talking and just looked at me. I didn't want to say anything, but with him looking at me the silence got uncomfortable, and I broke.

"So?" I said.

That was what he was waiting for. "So we're getting one," he said. "The judge is issuing it now. In the meantime, my cops are sitting down there, no one's going in and out, and we're sitting and waiting on a warrant. As soon as we get it we'll turn that place upside down. When we find that piece of paper you can go."

"Oh."

"Providing it corroborates your story."

I said nothing.

"In the meantime, we'd like you to stick around. You're not under arrest. You're doing it voluntarily, because you're a good citizen and you want to assist the police and do the right thing. At least that is my understanding of the situation. Of course, if I'm wrong, if you want to insist on enforcing your constitutional rights, then I'm sure that the same judge who's issuing the search warrant would find the evidence is sufficient to issue another kind of warrant, if you know what I mean. So if you decide you want to leave, just let me know."

I said nothing. There was nothing to say.

MacAullif nodded to the stenographer, who closed his notebook and got up. They went out, closing the door behind them.

For the first time since MacAullif dropped the bomb, I had time to think. And the first thought that sprang to mind was the same old adage: how bad is it going to be?

Pretty bad. What are the odds, I asked myself. What are the odds, when they find that piece of paper, that Wendy/Cheryl got the address right? I wouldn't have staked my life on it, and, basically, that was what I was doing. I mean, when they found that paper it was just as likely to say 309 as it was 307, or even some other number entirely.

And the thing is, it was all my fault. My only excuse was I'd never found a dead body before and I was terribly rattled. But, Jesus Christ. I mean, I knew how incompetent Wendy/Cheryl was. I knew practically every address they gave me was wrong. But I hadn't thought of that. I'd had the address and I'd given Leroy the address and he'd given Wendy/Cheryl the address, and I'd just assumed that would be that. But that wasn't the natural order of things. Leroy should have given her the address and she should have given me the address, and I should have written it down. And then I would have had the same address that she had, and my story would check. But it hadn't happened that way, so it didn't. And like a fool, I hadn't even listened to Wendy/Cheryl when she gave me the address on the phone.

It was small consolation to know that even if I had it wouldn't have done any good. She would have given me the wrong address, and I would have known it was the wrong address, but I couldn't have interrupted her and said, "Hey, you got the address wrong," cause how would I know? I'd have just had to take it—perhaps even change the address in my notebook—and then what? Pretend I'd called the guy and got the right address? Not on your life. The guy was obviously dead by that time. I wouldn't have wanted to open up that can of worms—claiming a nonexistent telephone conversation with a dead man. No. I'd have had to grit my teeth, go blundering into 309 West 127th Street, and try like hell to scare up some tenant who could tell me the guy I was looking for lived next door. Then I could have scrawled a 9 over the 7 in my notebook, then changed it *back* to a 7, and with luck the cops wouldn't be able to tell which number had been written first. Yeah. That might have worked.

I realized I was engaging in a lot of profitless speculation. I also realized the reason I was doing it was I was
fresh out of profitable speculation. As far as I was concerned, the die was cast. It was out of my hands. The
police would find the paper and it would either save
me or fuck me. And there was nothing I could do but
sit and wait.

I sat there for about an hour. Then MacAullif and
Daniels came in. I tried to read their faces, but I
couldn't. They looked grim, but, to me, cops always
look grim.

"All right," MacAullif said. "You can go."

I tried my best not to look as if I'd just gotten an
eleventh hour stay of execution from the governor. It
was hard. "You find the paper?" I said, casually.

"No."

"No?"

MacAullif shook his head. "No. We took that whole
office apart. We got a matron down there and searched
everyone to the skin. The paper is gone."

"What does that mean?"

"It means you can go. Without that paper, we don't
have sufficient evidence to arrest you. Not at the present time. But you'll be around. We checked up on you.
You got a wife and kid. You're not going anywhere.
We'll know where to find you."

"Hey, come on, Sergeant. What have I done?"

MacAullif took a deep breath and blew it out again.
"The paper is missing. As far as I'm concerned, that's
the most suspicious circumstance in the case."

I looked at him. "Give me a break. I've been sitting
here all afternoon. Whaddya think, I eluded the police

guard, rushed up to the office, and snatched the paper out from under the noses of the cops who were searching the place?"

"No, I don't. But your story doesn't hold up. Not without that paper. You claim it would corroborate your story. It could also disprove it. As far as I'm concerned, the most significant thing is that it's gone. I don't like that."

"I don't like it either."

"Good. Daniels here doesn't like it too much himself. So we're all in accord. We don't like it. At any rate, you can go."

"Great. What about my briefcase?"

"Downstairs at the front desk. You'll have to sign for it."

"O.K."

My beeper went off. I'd forgotten I was wearing it, and I jumped about a half a mile. MacAullif and Daniels never blinked. I shut it off.

"That'll be your office," MacAullif said, "telling you your boss wants to see you. He asked us to tell you he wanted you in his office as soon as you were through here. He was rather emphatic about it. Frankly, he didn't seem happy."

"I'll bet."

"O.K. That's it. You're free to go."

"That's fine," I said. "Except I was picked up in Harlem. Any chance of getting a ride back to pick up my car?"

MacAullif shrugged. "About as much chance as the Knicks have of making the playoffs."

I'm a sports fan. I didn't have to ask him what that meant.

I went out in the hall to the pay phone and called my office. Sure enough, Wendy/Cheryl told me Richard wanted to see me right away. I told her I'd be right there.

I went downstairs and picked up my briefcase. I checked out the contents before I signed for it. Apparently police corruption wasn't as bad as it was rumored to be, because my camera was still there.

I went outside to Chambers Street and caught the Lexington Avenue subway uptown. I didn't get off at 14th Street though. I was going to Richard's office all right, but I had a couple of stops to make first.

On the subway I started getting paranoid that maybe the cops were having me followed. I looked around, trying to spot the tail. The young guy in a suit strap-hanging about four people down the car looked like a plain clothes cop to me, at least he did until he got off at 23rd Street.

I got off at 42nd Street, shuttled to Times Square, and caught the Broadway 1-train uptown. I couldn't help thinking to myself, what kind of an asshole detective takes three subway trains uptown when there's something as important as the videotape evidence that might disappear any moment if he doesn't get to it in time? The answer, of course, was one with less than five bucks in his pocket who can't afford to take a cab.

I got off at 125th Street and walked down the elevated platform to the stairs. As far as I could see, I was the only white man who got off at the stop, but it occurred to me if they were gonna tail me through Harlem, they'd probably send a black man to do it.

I walked up to 127th and over to Darryl Jackson's apartment. My car was right out front where I'd left it. I looked around. There was no one in sight. Well, if they were tailing me, they were just too damn smart. I couldn't spot 'em. I just had to risk it.

I got in my car, switched off the code alarm, gunned the motor, and pulled out.

I drove around and pulled up right in back of the dumpster. Two teen-age kids were playing football in the street right next to it. They weren't wearing gloves and their fingers must have been falling off and how they were catching the ball was beyond me, but they were doing it. I wished they weren't. They were going to think I was pretty weird, but I couldn't help that. I got out of the car, walked over to the corner of the dumpster, jumped up, leaned my stomach on the side, and reached down.

I had expected to reach all the way down to the bottom, but my hands immediately encountered boards, plaster, nails, bags, and assorted other junk that had been dumped there in the course of the afternoon. Shit. Garbage—what a hell of a thing to put in a dumpster.

I began pawing my way through it, desperately trying to dig down to the bottom. I stole a look. The guys had stopped playing football and were standing there staring at me. I couldn't help that. I kept on digging.

I found it. A white plastic bag. I pulled it out, straightened up, and hopped down to the ground. I opened it and looked inside, just to make sure I hadn't grabbed a bag of Rice-a-Roni boxes by mistake. I hopped in my car and took off, leaving two very puzzled looking football players staring after the crazy honky.

11

IT WAS 5:15 by the time I got to Rosenberg and Stone. The office more or less shuts down at 5:00, but the switchboard stays open till 6:00, so Wendy and Cheryl were still there. I say Wendy and Cheryl rather than Wendy/Cheryl because in person I can tell them apart. Wendy looked like one of those girls you'd see at college whom you knew, on the one hand, would never get a date, but, on the other hand, would get a 98 on the psych final, and wreck the curve for everybody else. Only Wendy was a double-threat—both plain *and* dumb. Cheryl was not unattractive, and looked as if she might have been moderately intelligent. It was only when she opened her mouth and sounded just like Wendy that one realized there was no one home.

Both girls were in their early twenties, and both were obviously slated for better things. At least, I certainly hoped so. As far as I could see their only redeeming feature was that they were willing to work for the pittance Richard was willing to pay.

Wendy and Cheryl regarded me with hostile eyes,

which was not surprising, seeing as how they had both been strip-searched.

"Where's Richard?" I asked.

"In his office," Wendy said. She squeezed it out through clenched teeth.

I saw no reason to prolong the conversation. I ran the gauntlet between their two desks and walked across the office to Richard's door.

I was not looking forward to going in. If Wendy and Cheryl were any indication of the mood in the office, I was not in for a good time. And after all, they were only secretaries—Richard was the boss. And Richard was not easy to deal with, even under the best of circumstances. He was a little guy, but he made up for it by being intense and energetic, almost to the point of being hyper. Dealing with him was kind of like dealing with a high-strung nervous dog. He was all over the place, so you never knew what to expect, and you always had to be on your guard.

And above all, he was money-conscious. He could go berserk over a missing paper clip, so I could imagine how he was going to feel about the disruption of his entire office and the loss of half a day's work.

I opened the door and walked in. Richard was seated at his desk. Far from being irate, he seemed perfectly calm. His manner was casual, almost benevolent. He actually stood up when I came in.

"Stanley," he said. "Come in. Sit down."

I did, wondering what the fuck was going on.

Richard came around and sat on the edge of his desk. "The cops give you a hard time?" he asked.

"No. Not that bad."

"That's good. When the cops couldn't find the paper,

I was afraid they'd take it out on you. They definitely did not seem pleased."

"They weren't. A Sergeant MacAullif was particularly unhappy. In fact, he considers the disappearance of the paper the most significant aspect of the case."

"I know."

"In other words, Wendy/Cheryl strike again."

"That's one way of looking at it."

"What do you mean?"

Richard took a pen out of his jacket pocket and began tapping it on his hand. "The disappearance of that paper either screws you royally or saves your ass. Depending on what's written on it, of course."

I looked at him narrowly. "Why do you say that?"

"Well," Richard said. "Whatever else the facts of the case might show, it seems obvious that this fellow Darryl Jackson had been dead for some time."

"So?"

"Dead men seldom call up to engage my services," Richard said dryly.

"But it happened. Wendy/Cheryl got the call."

"There's no disputing that. I'm just stating that it is rather remarkable."

"So?"

"I'm just wondering if you've given any thought to what's going to happen when the cops find that paper."

I stared at him. "But they didn't find it. They gave up."

"They didn't find it, but they haven't given up. If you look on your way out you'll see there are cops combing the alley outside the building on the off chance some one tossed that paper out the window."

"You're kidding."

"I'm serious. Take a look."

I went to the window, opened it, and looked out. It was twelve stories down and it was dark, but I could see flashlights moving in the alley.

I closed the window, went back and sat down.

"O.K.," I said. "So they haven't given up."

"Right. So my question is, have you given any thought to what's going to happen when the cops find that paper?"

"Are you kidding. I've been sitting in the police station all afternoon with nothing to do *except* think of what's going to happen when they find that paper."

"And what have you come up with?"

"Nothing. I don't know."

"Well you should."

I was beginning to get annoyed. "All right. Fine. I should. But I don't. So you tell me. What's going to happen when the cops find that paper?"

"They won't," Richard said.

"Why not?"

Richard shrugged. Everyone seemed to be shrugging at me today. He reached into his jacket pocket and casually pulled out a folded piece of paper.

"Because I have it right here."

12

I'D ALWAYS KNOWN Richard was a good lawyer. He was only 30 years old, and in the short time he had been practicing, he had already built up a reputation among insurance adjusters as a demon negotiator. His record of exorbitantly high settlements was simply remarkable. Even more remarkable was the fact that, despite this, insurance adjusters were still willing to settle with him, rather than go to court. This was because, high as the settlements were, they were nothing compared to the judgments juries were awarding Richard's clients. As the word got around, the percentage of Richard's cases settled out of court was going steadily up. "Rosenberg? —Settle!" was a typical insurance company reaction. For, as good as Richard was at negotiation, he was better in court.

So far in the course of my business, I'd never been called upon to testify in court in any of Richard's cases, so I'd never really seen him in action. So I'd never known what the secret to his courtroom success really was. I learned it now. I learned it from the manner in which he produced the paper—casually, matter of

factly, but beautifully set up and perfectly timed. It was
nothing more than an elaborate grandstand—a bit of
business of the type that would dazzle a jury, pre-
formed in this case to an audience of one. Because, I
now realized, though no one would have ever suspected
it, this apparently unprepossessing man was, to all
intents and purposes, a showman.

And, as cheap and theatrical as the production of the
paper was, it was certainly effective.

I gawked at the paper, fascinated, just as a jury
would have been. I was so startled, I could think of
nothing to say, but Richard hadn't expected me to say
anything. He went on calmly, matter-of-factly, "When
the police examined the appointment log and discovered the address was wrong, I realized the significance
of it before they did. Of course, I'm more familiar with
the workings of my office. While the police were exam-
ining the log, I looked on Wendy's desk to see if the
scratch paper was there. It was lying right on top. I saw
at once that the address on it was also incorrect, and, of
course, I realized the implications. So while the police
were busy with the log I slipped the paper off the desk
and folded it up and put it in my pocket. Then, when
the police questioned me about the inconsistency in the
address, I immediately advanced the theory of the
piece of scratch paper from which the address had
been transferred to the log. The police, of course,
wanted the paper. When it was not discovered on either
Wendy or Cheryl's desk, and the police began to
broaden their search, I complained of the disruption to
my office, and raised the question of the warrant. Naturally, the police didn't have one. When I saw they were
determined to get one, I retired to my office, locked the

door, opened the window, took the paper, folded it into a paper airplane, and sailed it across the alley onto the roof of the building next door. The police then arrived with a warrant and instituted a painstakingly thorough search—as Wendy and Cheryl can attest—which eventually proved fruitless."

I sat staring at him, openmouthed. Under the circumstances, that was probably the wisest thing to do anyway.

"After the police had departed, I left the office, entered the building next door, obtained access to the roof, and retrieved the paper in question. On my way back I noted the presence of several policemen who, even now, are searching the alley to no avail."

He stopped and looked at me. I must say he looked pleased with himself, and I can't say I blamed him. Good lord.

It was several seconds before I was able to speak. When I could, only one word came to mind.

"Why?"

He looked at me in surprise. "Why what?"

"Why did you do it?"

He smiled and shook his head. "Why? The police were harassing you over an incident that occurred while you were in my employ. That makes you, for all intents and purposes, my client. And as an attorney, it is my duty to do everything I can to protect my client's interests. What kind of an attorney would I be if I let evidence of that kind fall into the hands of the police?"

I looked at him. That was an answer, but like the answers I'd given Daniels about the door, it was an answer that didn't explain. I still had no idea why he'd done it.

"Yes, but . . ."

"But what?"

"Well, look. I can understand your protecting my rights as a client and all that, but taking that paper is something else. Isn't that suppressing evidence?"

"Evidence? Evidence of what? Evidence that Wendy is incompetent, I suppose. But as far as the murder investigation is concerned, I fail to see how it could be considered evidence."

"A minute ago you said it *was* evidence."

Richard smiled. "You should have been an attorney. Should you become one, try to remember that facts are open to many interpretations, and you should always choose the one that gives you and your client the least amount of problems."

"Thanks for the tip."

"Don't mention it. Now then. Let's look at the alleged evidence. The police don't have the benefit of knowing what's on this piece of paper. I do. The address is wrong. Now then, would you like to explain to me how that happened?"

"No."

"Why don't you do it anyway? After all, I'm your attorney. You can tell me anything."

"I'm aware of the law regarding attorney/client privilege."

"Good. Then why don't you explain? It might be good practice for you, in case the police raise the point."

I'd been thinking like the devil and fighting for time. I'd just about used up my allotment. It was time to take a shot. "All right," I said. "You want a theory? How about this. Wendy took the call. She wrote down the address wrong. Then she beeped me and gave me the address. But she had *heard* the address right. So subconsciously she knew it. So when she read it off the paper she transposed it in her mind again and gave me the correct address. Later, when she transferred it into the log, she copied exactly what was on the paper."

"That's your explanation?"

"It's *an* explanation."

"It's a poor one."

"I can't help that. Got a better one?"

"No. So let's examine the case for a minute."

"Do we have to?"

"I think so. Seeing as how I've put myself in the position of being an accessory after the fact, I think you owe me that much."

I sighed. "All right. Shoot."

"After Wendy gave you the address, did you call up Darryl Jackson to verify it, and get no answer?"

I hesitated. Richard grinned. "Hadn't thought of that one, had you?"

"What do you mean, I hadn't thought of it? No one *asked* me it, if that's what you mean."

"And what's the answer?"

"The answer is no, I didn't. I was nearby, and I went right over there."

"That's what I thought."

Richard went back and sat down. He swiveled his chair around and put his feet up on his desk. "You see," he said. "It doesn't hold up."

"What?"

"Your story doesn't hold up. Even if the address were *right*, the story wouldn't hold up."

"Why not?"

Richard smiled. "You've been after me to fire Wendy and Cheryl for at least a month. Every time you come in here to drop off your cases you tell me how incompetent they are, how they can't get anything right, how every address they give you is wrong. Now the police may buy your story, but I don't. I just cannot believe, knowing how you feel about Wendy and Cheryl, that you would have gone over there without calling first to verify the address."

"But I did."

"I know. Therefore it becomes necessary to ask you a few more questions."

I shrugged. "Go ahead."

"Did you kill him?"

I smiled. Shook my head. "No. I did not."

"Then why did you go there?"

"You know why. Wendy beeped me—"

"Yes. Yes," he said impatiently. "Wendy beeped you and all the rest of it. I mean why did you *really* go?"

"I told you."

"Very well." Richard laced his fingers together, and pushed them out in front of him until the knuckles cracked. I think I winced. He brought his hands back up to his face, and rested his chin on his thumbs. "Despite the fact you say you didn't kill him," he said judiciously, "you may still be charged with the crime. Even without that piece of paper the police may feel they have sufficient evidence to build up a case. That depends, of course, on what your *real* relationship with Darryl Jackson actually was and whether the police are able to uncover it."

"I never met the man in my life."

"That doesn't matter. You could still be charged with the crime."

"So?"

"I could get you off."

"What?"

"If you killed him, I could get you off. Even if you didn't kill him, I could get you off. It would be harder, but I could still do it."

I stared at him. "What do you mean, if I didn't kill him it would be harder?"

"If you killed him, we'd know exactly what the facts were, and we could explain 'em away. It'd be a snap. If you didn't kill him, we're liable to run into a few surprises."

"I didn't kill him."

"Too bad."

Richard picked up a pen and began doodling on a legal notepad. "Nonetheless, this might be a good time to tell me all about it."

"There's nothing to tell."

He stopped doodling, put down the pen. "Very well. We'll see. Circumstances may alter. You might change your mind."

There was genuine regret in Richard's voice, and suddenly I understood the situation. Richard's actions, his attitude, his stealing the paper, the whole thing. He was treating me nicely because he was treating me as a client rather than an employee. But more than that, he was treating me as a *prospective* client. He was *wooing* me as a client. He'd been attempting to impress me with his ability, to show me how wise I'd be to let him represent me in this matter. And having realized this, I also realized why.

We all have our daydreams. Mine is making my acceptance speech at the Academy Awards, hypocritically thanking all the little people, people who, if the truth be known, were too stupid to recognize my talent and had thrown roadblocks in my path all the way, and whom I had actually triumphed in *spite* of.

And this was Richard's. Standing in front of the jury in a packed courthouse in a sensational murder trial, and conducting brilliant cross-examinations, and getting his client off.

I never would have thought it of him. As long as I'd known Richard, his only motivation had always been money. But then why shouldn't he have daydreams like anybody else?

And I had to ruin his.

"I doubt it, Richard. I'm really not involved."

"Very well," Richard said. He swung his feet down from the desk. His manner changed, and he became, once again, the boss.

But with a slight difference. It was barely perceptible, but it was there. Richard was just a touch more formal and rigid than usual, which gave him the air of a rejected suitor.

He opened the desk drawer and pulled out a folded paper. "In that case, you won't mind the work," he said somewhat stiffly. "This subpoena has to be served in Brooklyn tonight." He shoved it across the desk. "Just drop it off on your way home."

13

ONCE AGAIN, Pamela Berringer sat on my living room couch.

It was 8:10 that evening. After leaving Richard's, I'd gone to a pay phone, called my wife, and told her to get Pamela Berringer over to our apartment on any pretext whatsoever and keep her there until I arrived. I hadn't told her why.

Then I'd rushed out to Bedford Stuyvesant and served the subpoena. I'd been lucky in finding the party home, and luckier still in that he was an old man who didn't want to push my face in when he found out why I was there.

I'd hurried home to discover that my wife had, indeed, succeeded in snaring Pamela Berringer. The pretext she'd given Ronnie had been that Tommie needed a playdate, so she had brought Joshua along with her. He and Tommie were happily playing Voltron in the other room.

So now, here we were again. Pamela seated on the couch, my wife seated next to her, and me across from them, just as we'd been before. It was hard to believe it had only been this morning. So much had happened since then.

I wondered how much of it Pamela knew.

"I went to see Darryl Jackson," I said.

My wife and Pamela both looked at me. There was a pause.

"Yes?" Pamela said.

"Yes." I said.

I waited. I didn't know what the situation was, but I wasn't giving anything away. I was watching Pamela carefully, to try to read her reactions. It wasn't easy. She seemed nervous, but, under the circumstances, she *would* be nervous, whether she knew about the murder or not.

"Well, what did he say?" she asked.

"He didn't say anything. He was dead."

Pamela and Alice gasped. They gawked at me open-mouthed. I knew it was genuine on my wife's part, but on Pamela's I wasn't sure.

I went on, "He was lying there on the floor with a large carving knife in his back. He was dead."

My wife recovered first. "My god! Stanley. Dead? Who killed him?"

I shrugged. "I don't know. The police seem to be inclined to think I did."

"What?!"

"I'm kidding, of course. The thing is, I found the body, which puts me at the scene of the crime. So right now I'm their only suspect."

"You found the body!" Alice said. "Jesus Christ, you mean you walked in there and found the body? What the hell were you doing, walking into that apartment? What the hell did you think you were doing? And the police think you're a suspect! My god, I can't believe it. I—"

I hadn't taken my eyes off Pamela. "Shut up," I said.
Alice gasped. I didn't talk to her that way.

"I'm sorry," I said, "but we haven't got much time.
Pamela's gotta get home. She can't keep Joshua up
much longer without old Ronnie getting suspicious. But
before she goes, I gotta get the facts. Now, what happened this morning after I left here?"

"What do you mean?" Alice asked.

"What time did you leave here, Pamela?"

"I don't know. It was around 11:30, quarter to
twelve."

I turned to Alice. "Is that right?"

Pamela started. "Hey, what are you doing, checking
up on me?"

"You're damn right I'm checking up on you. This is a
murder case, and I gotta be sure of my facts. Now is
that when she left?"

"I think so. It was around then."

"Fine. Where did you go?"

Pamela bristled. "You can't question me like some
common criminal."

She was acting indignant, probably because it was
the easiest thing for her to act. But I could see through
it. And what I saw was fear.

Unfortunately, I was in no position to be sympathetic.

"Oh yeah," I said. "Well, the police can. And if I don't
get some answers right fast you're going to be talking to
them. This is a murder case, and if the police can't find
anybody else to pick on, they're going to pick on me.
So I want some answers."

Her eyes darted around the room. I could see her
mind going. "All right," she said. "I went shopping."

"Alone?"

"Yes, alone."

"What'd you buy?"

"I didn't buy anything. I was just looking."

"Then you can't prove it."

"What?"

"What stores did you go to? Any of the clerks remember you?"

"Hey, what is this?"

"What do you think it is? It's a murder interrogation. Now what stores did you go to?"

"Stores on Broadway. I don't remember which ones."

"Great. I don't suppose you happened to call on Darryl Jackson in the course of your travels?"

She looked at me. "Why would I do that?"

I shrugged. "It's not an illogical move. We'd just had a long conversation about that tape. I didn't impress you very much. You thought my chances of recovering it were slim. So you thought you'd give it one last shot."

"Well, I didn't."

"All right. Ever been to his apartment?"

"Why?"

"I want to know. You obviously have, since you gave me his address."

"All right, so I've been there. So what?"

"Then your fingerprints will be there. That, coupled with the videotape, would be enough to make you suspect number one."

She kept quiet, thinking that over.

"Well," I said. "Don't you want to ask me any questions?"

"I don't understand. What do you mean? You've been asking *me* questions."

"Right, but we got a break in the action here. And I

would think normal curiosity might lead one to ask, was I alone when I found the body? Did I look around any? Had the apartment been searched? You know. Stuff like that."

"Well," Pamela said. "Had it?"

"It had not only been searched, it had been ransacked. Apparently someone was looking for that tape."

"Did they find it?"

"It would appear not. The place was totally trashed."

"I see."

"So, that's the situation. Darryl Jackson was your pimp. He was also blackmailing you. Now he's dead. Your fingerprints are all over that apartment. Under the circumstances, while you may not think so, it seems to me it would be a hell of a good idea for you to figure out just where the hell you were this afternoon."

She looked at me. Bit her lip. Said nothing.

It was around 8:30 when Pamela Berringer finally left. I figured that was the outside limit to which we could stretch Ronnie's credulity about keeping two 5-year-old kids up on a school night.

What followed was one of the longest evenings of my life. That's because what I really wanted to do was get down to my office and take a look at those video tapes. I'd dropped them off there on my way down to Richard's. That's because, though I may be dumb, I'm not stupid. With my luck, if I'd left them in the car it would have been burglarized, stolen, or towed. At any rate, the tapes were there, and I couldn't go there because I couldn't think of any legitimate excuse to get out of the house, and I wasn't about to tell Alice the real reason. Marriage may be a partnership, but in my book that doesn't include making your partner an accessory to suppressing evidence in a murder case. Besides, Alice was standing in with Pamela, and I couldn't trust her not to let the information slip.

I know I should have told Pamela I had the tapes. After all, she was vitally concerned, and she was the one who had asked me to get them in the first place. But if she knew I had them, she wouldn't want me to see them, and she'd want to destroy them. And I couldn't let her do that. The situation had changed materially since this morning. Before it was just blackmail. Now it was murder.

Besides, for all intents and purposes, my obligation to Pamela Berringer was over. Darryl Jackson's death had left her sitting pretty. Unless she killed him—and I couldn't discount the possibility—her troubles were over. Mine were just beginning.

So I couldn't let her have the tapes. She'd have destroyed them to protect her reputation. That's a hell of a good motivation, but my motivation for keeping them was slightly better. I just might need them to squirm out from under a murder rap.

Alice and I put Tommie to bed. Then Alice subjected me to an interrogation only ten times worse than the one I'd given Pamela Berringer. I told her everything except about the tapes, and about the address that didn't match. I saw no reason to worry her about that. I mean, one hysterical paranoid person to a family is quite enough, thank you very much.

It was well after midnight when we finally got to bed. I lay down and turned out the light, because there was nothing else that I could do, but I knew it was going to be a long time before I'd be able to get to sleep.

14

I READ THE NEW YORK POST on the subway on my way to the office the next morning. I was looking for the story of the murder of Darryl Jackson, but I couldn't find it. Apparently the murder of a black pimp in Harlem didn't even rate a headline. I was nearly to Times Square when I finally stumbled across it on the one page where I hadn't even thought to look—the crack page. It was lumped together with two other murders, one in the Bronx and one in Queens. There were no details, just the name and address and the fact that he had been stabbed. The Post, one-up on Wendy/Cheryl, had gotten the address right. The assailant was described as, "Probably a crack addict."

The brevity of the story allowed me to finish the article before the train pulled into Times Square. I kept my hand pressed firmly against my wallet in my front pants pocket, made my way through the station, and emerged on the corner of 7th Avenue and 42nd Street. I looked around for a video tape rental store. I found one a couple of blocks up the street. Alice and I had a VCR, but I couldn't bring it down to the office without tipping her off to the situation, so I had to rent one.

Renting one, I discovered, was actually pretty cheap. They let me have it for $4.95. The only catch was, you had to put down a hundred dollar deposit. Fortunately, you could do it on your Master Charge, and it didn't cost you anything, because they just filled out the slip, and then tore it up when you brought the machine back. They did check, however, to see if the card was good for a hundred dollars, which would have been a problem, seeing as how I'm always charged to the limit, except the Master Charge people, in their infinite greed, had just raised my limit again, up to twenty-five-hundred dollars.

The guy in the store seemed a little nonplussed that I wanted to rent a machine without a tape, but I assured him I had a tape.

"In fact, I've got six of them," I told him.

At any rate, he let me do it.

I took the machine, went out, hunted up an electronics store, and bought the cheapest black and white television set I could find that could get a picture on any channel. The reception didn't matter, of course, as I was only going to use it as a monitor.

I carried the whole mess up to 47th Street to the small office my father-in-law still carried on the books of the Cohen Bag Company, but let me use for my business. I took the elevator up to the third floor, and walked down the hall to the door with the plaque reading, STANLEY HASTINGS DETECTIVE AGENCY that had been given me by friends as a joke. I opened the door, carted the stuff inside, and put it down.

The mail had already arrived. It had been pushed

through the slot and was lying just inside the door. It was all bills, so I let it lie. Instead, I picked up the bag of video tapes that was lying next to it. I'd been parked illegally downstairs when I'd left it there the night before, so I'd just flung it in the door and raced back to catch the elevator before it left the floor, and by some miracle had managed to get back to my car before it was either ticketed or towed.

I took the bag of video tapes and set it on my desk. I took out the TV and the VCR and set 'em up. When I turned the TV on all I got was loud static, but that's all you get without a tape.

I opened the plastic bag and took out the six cassettes. I saw now what I hadn't noticed before—one of them was slightly different. As I say, we have a VCR, so I knew something about video tapes. Five of them were of the cheapest quality you can buy. The sixth was of a higher grade. So I tried that one first.

I put it in the VCR and pushed play. There was the usual introductory static and flashing. Then the picture cleared up and I could see the camera was focused on a king-sized bed. It was well lit. Production values, as they say in the movie biz, were excellent.

A girl entered the frame. It was Pamela Berringer. She was dressed in a red satin sheath. She took it off. Underneath she had on black lace underwear. She took that off too.

She got on the bed and proceeded to disport herself in a variety of positions, all of which seemed to feature wide-spread legs. When she got up on all fours, arched her backside to the camera, reached back, pulled the cheeks of her ass open, and looked over her shoulder with an arch, aren't-I-being-naughty look, I realized I was going to have a tough time meeting her eyes at our next detective/client conference.

I also realized I had a raging hardon. What does Mike Hammer do in these situations? Beat off? Hire a hooker? I didn't know.

I shut off the VCR, and walked around the office a bit. I took a page out of Woody Allen's book, and thought about baseball players. I'm originally from Massachusetts, so I thought about Dwight Evans and Jim Rice. That seemed to do the trick.

I switched the tape back on. I used the fast-forward search to speed through the rest of Pamela's performance.

A man joined her on the bed. I slowed back to normal speed to get a look at him. He didn't seem particularly handsome, but he was certainly well-endowed. At any rate, Pamela seemed glad to see him. She took his cock and proceeded to suck on it. When it was good and ready, she lay on her back on the bed and he plunged it into her.

He fucked her like that for a couple of minutes. Meanwhile, the camera moved around and zoomed in and out, to show every aspect of the operation to the best advantage.

Then he pulled out, flipped her over on her hands and knees, and stuck his cock up her ass. He fucked her up the ass while the camera went through the same business.

He pulled out, flipped her over again, straddled her, and rubbed his cock back and forth between her breasts. Finally he came in her face.

O.K. . . . .

It was hard to take, all right. I'd known she made the

tape. I'd known what I was going to see. And I knew she'd been forced into it. I knew she'd really had no choice.

But still.

The tape ended. I switched it off, and put it on rewind. It was still rewinding when my beeper went off. I went to the phone and called Rosenberg and Stone.

"Agent 005," I said when they answered.

Wendy/Cheryl must have still been mad at me, because she didn't call me by name. "I have a new case for you," she said shortly.

I took out my notebook and wrote down the information, right after the entry about Darryl Jackson: a Matilda Mae Smith on Martin Luther King Boulevard in Jersey City, New Jersey. I knew one thing for sure. I was damn well gonna call and verify *this* address.

But I couldn't The client had no phone. Wendy/-Cheryl had made the appointment for me for between 11:00 and 12:00.

I was getting fed up with the coldshoulder I was getting. After all, *I* hadn't gotten Darryl Jackson's address wrong. So I said, "If there's no phone, I sure hope *this* address is correct."

"It should be," Wendy/Cheryl said acidly. "I had her repeat it three times. How many times would you like it?"

I settled for twice, along with me reading it back to her. I figured by then I had what she had, and if she had it wrong, there was nothing I could do about it anyway.

I hung up. I switched off the VCR, which had finished rewinding the tape, and the TV. I ejected the tape and put it back in its box. I would have liked to have checked out the other five, but it was nearly 10:30, and seeing as how the client had no phone, I had to get there.

I checked my answering machine for messages, which I'd neglected to do before, and was gratified to see there were none. I left it switched on. I grabbed my briefcase, and went out.

Jersey City is not far from midtown if you go through the Lincoln Tunnel, but, of course, I had left my car uptown rather than pay the 15 to 20 bucks it would have cost me to park near the office. Since some days I don't make much more than that, midtown parking is one luxury I never afford.

I took the subway back uptown, picked up my car, and headed out. I got on the West Side Highway and headed uptown for the George Washington Bridge. It's a little longer getting to Jersey City that way, but a hell of a lot easier than fighting my way back down to the Lincoln Tunnel through midtown traffic.

I got off the Jersey Pike and headed into Jersey City. I don't have a Hagstrom Map of Jersey City, so I had to drive around a little before I found Martin Luther King Drive. When I did, I checked which way the numbers were running, checked Matilda Mae Smith's address, and hung a left.

The closer I got to Matilda Mae Smith's, the worse the neighborhood got. Abandoned, cinderblocked-up buildings, wooden-frame houses all but falling down, rubble-filled empty lots. Garbage everywhere. And I couldn't help wondering, as I always did in these circumstances, why it was every time people had some great black leader they wanted to honor, they took some god-awful slum street and named it after him.

The answer, as always, was both obvious and sad: because that's where the black people live.

The address I wanted turned out to be a four-story frame house that appeared to be the only occupied building on the block, the others having been either gutted, boarded up, or knocked down. I pulled up in front of it, took my briefcase, and got out.

The front door was locked, and there was no buzzer or bell. Since the client had no phone, I had no recourse but to go back out in the street and shout her name at the windows above.

"Matilda Mae Smith," I bellowed. I waited a few seconds, then bellowed again.

A couple of guys came down the street and looked at me as if I were something weird. I can't say as I blamed them. I felt like a fool.

But the thing is, the motivation I'd told Daniels about only getting paid when a case was done happened to be true. And having driven all the way to Jersey, I was damned if I was going to wash the trip out and put it on a "pend" sheet. So I kept on shouting.

A window on the third floor opened and a skinny black kid about eight stuck his head out.

"You the lawyer?" he called down.

I wasn't going to debate the point with an 8-year-old kid.

"Yes," I yelled back.

"Just a minute," he said. "I'll throw you the key."

His head disappeared and returned a minute later. His arm reached out and I could see a key ring gleaming in his hand. He tossed it to me. I reached for it, and it glanced off my hand and landed on the sidewalk. I picked it up, realizing I'd just plummeted in his estimation.

I opened the door and went in. The kid was waiting for me at the top of the stairs on the third floor.

"In here," he said, and led me into the apartment.

It was a small two-room apartment, barely furnished at all. The room we entered was a living room-kitchen combination. Aside from an old worn easy chair, the kitchen appliances, which looked suspiciously as if they hadn't functioned in years, were the only furnishings in the room. Through a door in the far wall I could see into the bedroom, where some mattresses and blankets on the floor seemed to be the only furnishings.

But the apartment was certainly occupied. There were so many kids of various ages that I couldn't be sure how many there actually were. I threaded my way through them to where a woman sat in the lone chair. She was a plump, black woman about 40. She was obviously in some pain.

"Matilda Mae Smith?" I said.

"Yes?"

"I'm Mr. Hastings, from the lawyer's office."

"Yes," she said. "I'm sorry, but I can't get up. And there are no other chairs."

"Don't worry, that's quite all right," I told her. I sat on the floor next to her, and opened my briefcase. "Just let me get my papers out here a minute." I took out a sign-up kit, and pulled out the fact sheet. Then I took out a clipboard, and rested the fact sheet on it. I pulled a pen out of my jacket pocket. "O.K.," I said, as I do at the start of every signup. "How did this happen to you?"

"There was a fire," she said.

I liked her for that. So many of my clients, when I ask that question say something like, "Well, I was at work, and then I got off work, and I was gonna go home, but

I was kinda hungry, so I went to this pizza place for a slice of pizza, you know, and the thing is I had to meet my friend to go to the movies, so . . .", and I sit there with my pen poised over the fact sheet waiting to hear something I can write down and wanting to strangle them. But Matilda Mae Smith went right for it.

"A fire?" I said. "Tell me about it."

She did. She and her children had been asleep in her old apartment. She had woken up about 2:00 in the morning and smelled smoke. She had run to the door and opened it. There was fire on the stairs. The whole building was going up. She was on the third floor and she couldn't get out. She had no phone to call for help. She had woken the kids, gone to the window and yelled for help.

Two men passing by heard her and saw the fire. One ran to call the fire department. The other stayed to help. There was no time to wait for the firemen. Matilda Mae Smith had taken her kids, one at a time, and thrown them into the arms of the stranger down below. Then she had jumped.

The man had been able to catch the kids. But she was heavy. She knocked him down. He was all right, but she broke her hip.

I took it all down carefully, particularly the part about the firemen and the ambulance and the hospital and the broken hip. It was an excellent case for Richard, better than his usual trip and fall. And more deserving, too.

"Were there smoke alarms?" I asked.

She snorted. "Are you kidding?"

"And no fire escapes?"

"No."

"Who owns the building, the City?"

"No. Slum landlord. Name of Gerald Baines."

Better and better. A private landlord. The case wouldn't have to go through the endless delays involved in suing the City. I took down the name and address of the landlord, then went back to the top of the fact sheet for the personal information that I always leave for last. I took down her name, address, age, date of birth, and social security number.

"Married or single?"

"Single."

"How many children do you have?"

"Eight."

That was even more than I'd estimated. It turned out three of them were grown up and lived elsewhere. The five that lived with her ranged from two to ten. I took down all their names, birth dates, and social security numbers.

"Were you employed before this happened?" I asked her.

I expected a no. A single woman with five dependent kids would be on public assistance. But she surprised me.

"Yes, I was," she said.

"Oh? What did you do?"

"I was the super in my building."

Shit.

The thing about my job is, you can't get involved. I learned that early on. You have to harden yourself. Not let it get to you. Or you'd go nuts.

Matilda Mae Smith was the super in her old building. I'd had similar cases before, so I knew that, technically, that made this a workman's compensation case, which meant there was no personal injury liability. Richard wouldn't touch it with a ten-foot pole.

The thing about the clients I deal with is that a lot of them are lazy, good-for-nothings trying to cash in on an injury, but some of them legitimately need help. And some of them, like Matilda Mae Smith, need *real* help, not the kind of help Richard or I could give her, even if the case had been legit. They don't need some settlement eighteen to twenty-four months down the road. They need help *now*. They need somebody to fight for them, to work for them, to take their side. Not to offer the tiny services that I render. I mean, what the hell do I do for these people? Nothing. I sign 'em to retainers, turn in my time sheets, and collect my money. And that's it. After the initial visit, I'm gone. And if the client should get a settlement some two years from now, I won't even know it. But that's the way it is. That's the nature of the job. That's all Richard and I can do.

And in this case, we couldn't even do that. Because the law said we couldn't. And the law's fucked. And Richard's fucked. And I'm fucked. And that's just the way it is.

I said nothing to Matilda Mae Smith, of course. I just filled out the fact sheet, had her sign the retainers, and got the hell out of there.

In the car, I stopped and wrote the case down on my paysheet: two hours and twenty-three miles. The fact that the case was no good made no difference—I'd still get paid for it. Yeah, two hours and twenty-three miles on my paysheet. That's all Matilda Mae Smith meant to me, and all she could mean to me. Cause the one thing about my job is, you can't let yourself care.

15

ON MY WAY BACK from Jersey I began to lose it. This
was not surprising. After all, it was less than twenty-
four hours ago that I'd found a dead body. Since then
I'd suppressed evidence, lied to the police, refused to
explain to my boss, held out on my wife, interrogated a
member of our car pool, viewed a porno flick, and carried out business as usual for Richard as if nothing had
happened. I know TV detectives can do all that without
it phasing them in the least, but believe me, I was worn
pretty thin. So it wasn't really surprising that I cracked
up, but rather that I held out that long.

I was coming into the toll plaza for the George
Washington Bridge. The car in front of me had a
BABY ON BOARD! sign. And I thought, Jesus Christ,
another one. I mean, forget the mentality that thinks the
way to protect their kids is to obscure the driver's vision
out the rear window. What gets me is the obvious
implication of the sign—that if I *don't* have a BABY
ON BOARD! it's perfectly all right to tail-gate me,
side-swipe me, and run me off the road.

And then I thought, Schmuck. What the hell are you

doing? Every damn stand-up comic in the world is doing BABY ON BOARD! routines, you dotta do one too?

And that's when I realized, I wasn't just thinking all this, I was saying it. I was talking to myself. Out loud.

I do that sometimes, because I'm a writer, and when I'm composing something, I will often say it out loud to see how it sounds. But that's different, because I'm doing it for a purpose, and I know I'm doing it.

But sometimes, when the pressure gets too much for me, I'll start doing it without knowing I'm doing it. And that's when I realize I'm starting to lose it.

I realized it now. And I started cracking up. Jesus Christ, here I am on my way back to my office to view a whole bunch of porno tapes in the hope of beating a murder rap, and I'm talking to myself and doing BABY ON BOARD! routines.

I was giggling so hard by the time I hit the toll booth I was barely able to ask for a receipt. The tool booth attendant, who obviously didn't get the joke, gave me a funny look, but still accepted my money.

I laughed my way over the George Washington Bridge and onto the West Side Highway. I had more or less calmed down by the time I took the exit at 96th Street. I parked my car, and took the subway back downtown to my office.

My beeper went off as I was unlocking my office. Shit. Of all the luck. Normally I wouldn't go back to my office after finishing a case, because it meant leaving my car all the way uptown. And then if I got beeped I'd have to go back and get it. But today I needed to see those tapes, so I had, and, sure enough, the minute I get here, beep, beep, beep, beep, beep.

I shut the damn thing off. Screw it. If the client has a phone, I'll stall them till tonight if I have to, but I'm going to see those tapes.

I called the office. Wendy/Cheryl answered the phone.

"Rosenberg and Stone."

"Agent 005."

"Stanley?"

Well, that was progress. Back to first-name basis.

"Yeah. You got a case?"

"Yes I do," she said.

She said it nicely. That bothered me. She was too nice. Almost smug.

"Well, what is it?"

"A murder."

"A murder? Who's the client?"

"You are."

"What!?"

"A Sergeant MacAullif called and asked me to beep you. He wants you in his office immediately. He was most insistent."

16

"**S**HUT UP."

I hadn't said a word. But I was about to. And Sergeant MacAullif had known it, despite the fact that he was standing with his back to me. I found that rather unsettling.

We were alone in MacAullif's office. He had brought me in and told me to sit down. Now he was standing looking out the window. I had no idea why I was there. Or rather, I had a lot of ideas, and none of them were very good. I would have liked to have asked, but MacAullif had told me to shut up, and under the circumstances, shutting up seemed a pretty good idea.

MacAullif turned around, put his hands on the back of his chair, and looked at me.

"I don't want you to talk," he said. "I want you to listen."

That was fine by me. I wasn't looking forward to any part of the interview, but if the Sergeant wanted me to listen, I'd listen. I had a feeling I wasn't going to like what I heard, but listening seemed a damn sight easier than answering questions.

MacAullif leaned on the chair, raised his eyes from me, and looked around the room. His eyes wandered over the pictures and certificates on the wall, as if looking for something. I realized he wasn't looking at anything in particular. He just had something to say, and was trying to figure out how to begin.

Finally he did.

"I don't believe in coincidence," he said.

There was a long pause. I opened my mouth.

"Shut up," he said. "I told you, I don't want you to talk." He took a breath, let it out again. "Three months ago you were in here with a bullet. A bullet connected with a murder case. Now you're here again. Involved in another murder case. You have a perfectly plausible story to account for your presence. At least, you would have if a secretary hadn't copied down a wrong address. Still, with the paper missing, your story might stand up. Me, I don't buy it at all."

I opened my mouth again.

"I told you to shut up. What is it Chuck Norris says in the movie? When I want your opinion I'll beat it out of you." MacAullif afforded himself a brief chuckle. "All right," he said. "Take the Albrect murder. That's the guy who got killed in that parking lot, in case you didn't know. You come in with a bullet and a story about finding it that's just about as plausible as the one about the missing piece of paper. A week later a guy shows up and confesses. He has a written confession that's been typed on five different typewriters. When we question him about it, it turns out there's a lot of stuff in it that he couldn't possibly have known. But it doesn't matter, cause there's enough in it to justify a warrant. And when we serve it, damned if we don't find the murder weapon and all the evidence we need, all tied up neat and tidy just waiting for us. And the thing is, when we arrest these guys, they all start singing and blaming it on each other, but each and every one of them swears the gun was a plant. But it doesn't matter, 'cause the confession stands up enough to justify the warrant, and that means the warrant stands up, and that means the evidence was obtained legally, and that means these guys are going down. Now the other cops say these guys are just lying about the murder weapon being a plant. But I keep thinking about that bullet. And to me, the whole affair reeks of just one thing: gifted amateur."

Sergeant MacAullif was a master of sarcasm, and what he did with the word "gifted" was a wonder to behold. I opened my mouth.

"Do I have to tell you again?" MacAullif said.

MacAullif took his hands off the chair and started pacing, which wasn't easy, his office being so small. He came back to the chair again.

"I'm a sergeant," he said. "I've been a sergeant for seventeen years. I'd like to be a lieutenant, but I probably never will. You know why? Because I don't play the game. I don't know how. I don't know how to kiss ass, and diddle the media, and say the right things, and do all those things you're supposed to do to uphold the glory of the N.Y.P.D. Quite frankly, I don't want to know how. I don't care about it. I don't give a shit. You know?"

He paused. Looked around. "I got a murder on my hands. I want it solved. And more than that. I don't just want it solved. I want the fucker who did it in jail." He shook his head. Smiled. "There's a difference, you know? Just between you and me I'd like to hang

Miranda up by his fucking balls, you know what I mean? Our legal system is a joke. There's mass murderers walking around today because some cop violated their civil rights by not informing them killing people was a crime, and if they did it again they were liable for arrest.

"Now, as far as I'm concerned, you have to fight back. And if a guy is guilty, I mean really guilty, I don't care what it takes to send the fuck to jail."

He paused and looked at me. "Which brings me to you."

He paused again and took a breath. "I don't peg you for this murder."

I would have liked to have thanked him with all my heart, but having been told four or five times to shut up, I held my peace.

"Before you start rejoicing, I should tell you the other cops do. But that's really because they got nobody else. But I don't peg you for it. And if you did it, and I can't get you for it, dumb as you are, well then you deserve to get away."

He took out a cigar and stuck it in his mouth.

"Don't worry," he said. "I'm not going to light it. I used to smoke 'em, but my doctor made me quit. Now I just chew on the end."

He took it out of his mouth and looked at me. "So why are you here? You're here because I don't believe in coincidence. Now I'm not asking you to talk, because you wouldn't tell me anything anyway, and, frankly, I don't care. But I think you're involved in this thing, and I think you were involved in the Albrect thing. And that's why I'm doing what I'm going to do. And it happens to be the type of thing I've been talking to you about, the type of thing that goes against the police department line and is going to keep me a sergeant all my life.

"Because, I figure, if you're not involved in this, if you're just some stupid innocent bystander, well, what's the harm? It's not going to matter anyway. But if I'm right, and a week or two from now some asshole comes in here and confesses to this crime, well, I don't care how it happened, or why it happened, I'm just glad it did."

He studied the end of his cigar for a moment, then looked back up at me.

"So I'm gonna tell you what we know."

17

SOMETIMES YOU FEEL GOOD, and sometimes you feel bad, and sometimes you just don't know. I guess that's why the word "ambivalent" was invented. That word had never been more appropriate to describe my feelings than it was now. I was overjoyed that Sergeant MacAullif didn't consider me a murder suspect. I was delighted that he didn't want to interrogate me. And I was quite pleased that I was about to find some things out about the Darryl Jackson murder that I needed to know. But I was shocked and dismayed to find out he was doing it because he thought I had meddled in the Albrect murder. I had, but he wasn't supposed to know it. I thought I was free and clear on that one. I thought I'd covered my tracks pretty well. And all the time, all the moves that I had thought were so clever, he had immediately recognized as the bumbling attempts of a gifted amateur. And the emotion that stirred in me was a primary one—at least a primary one for me. And that emotion was fear. That cold, clammy feeling that someone is looking right through you, and knows all about you, and knows what you think.

I had no time to dwell on it, however, for MacAullif

was already taking a folder off his desk and pulling papers out of it.

"Let's start with the autopsy report," he said. He held up the paper and read from it. "Death was due to a laceration from a sharp object entering the back and perforating the left ventricle, etc., etc., bullshit, bullshit." He lowered the paper. "We know all that. He got stabbed with a knife. Now, the time element. The medical examiner's covering his ass like crazy. He puts the time of death at somewhere between eleven o'clock and one thirty. That's pretty gutless, under the circumstances, seeing as how your call was logged in at 1:27. But that's what happens when the lawyers start chewing the shit out of the legal system. This guy's been on the stand before, and he knows if he made the outside limit 1:15, some wise-ass lawyer would make him look like a damn fool for saying the murder couldn't have taken place at 1:*16*, so there you are. 1:30 is a pretty safe outside limit, seeing as how the radio patrol cops got there by 1:35. At any rate, that's what the spineless fuck has done, and that leaves you right in the middle of it.

"Just between you and me, the murder probably took place somewhere between 12:00 and 1:00, which would almost let you out of it, but we have to live with what we get."

MacAullif looked at me. "Any comments?"

"I thought you didn't want me to talk."

"Naw, I just didn't want you to lie to me about how you're not involved. I don't want to hear it. We're discussing the case now. Let's discuss it."

"All right. What do you want to discuss?"

"The time of death. When do you think he was killed?"

"Before I got there."

MacAullif looked at me. "Don't be smart. This is a limited-time offer, and it may be withdrawn. When do you think he was killed?"

"I don't know. I just know it couldn't have been too long before I got there, cause when I saw the body there was still blood coming from the wound."

"And what time was that?"

"That I got there?"

"Yeah."

I realized the difference between this discussion and an interrogation was not bigger than a breadbox.

"Didn't you say the police logged my call at 1:27?"

"Yeah. And how long was that after you found the body?"

"I don't know. A matter of minutes."

"How many minutes?"

"I don't know. Three or four."

"Three or four minutes? And what were you doing for that long?"

"Throwing up in the bathroom."

"Ah, yes. All right, let's put this together. How long were you knocking on the door before you got into the apartment?"

"I don't know. Five, ten minutes."

He shook his head. "Don't be silly. Nobody stands in the hallway for five or ten minutes banging on a door. It may seem a long time, but you figure three, four minutes tops."

I shrugged. "If you say so."

"I do."

"All right. Say three or four minutes."

"Then you opened the door."

"Right."

"You saw the apartment had been ransacked, so you went in."

"That's right."

"You say you went in to see if anything had happened to Darryl Jackson."

"That's right. I did."

"Did you search the apartment?"

"No."

"I didn't think you had. Because, after all, you weren't looking for anything. You were just trying to find Darryl Jackson."

"That's right."

"So, as soon as you saw he wasn't in the living room, you went in the bedroom."

"Yes."

"And found the body."

"That's right."

"That couldn't have taken more than a minute."

"No, I guess not."

"And we have just determined that was three or four minutes before you called the cops."

"That's just a rough estimate."

"Yeah, but it's a pretty good one. Anything more than that would seem excessive."

"So?"

"So, let's put it together. Your call was logged at 1:27. You found the body three or four minutes before that. That's 1:23, 1:24. You found the body within a minute of entering the apartment. That's 1:22, 1:23. You got into the apartment after three or four minutes of pounding on the door. That puts your arrival at the apartment no earlier than 1:18."

"If you say so."

"Well, it couldn't have been any earlier than that. Because Wendy Millington puts the time she beeped you at approximately 1:15."

"I wouldn't take her word for anything."

"Neither would I. But I have to accept the facts as I get 'em, and that's a fact."

"That she beeped me at 1:15?"

"No. That she says she did."

"O.K. In any case, her story corroborates mine. What's the point?"

"A Mr. Claude Phillips, from the adjoining apartment, told the police, and I quote—" He grabbed a sheaf of papers, flipped through them, found what he was looking for. "Some dumb-ass honky motherfucker bang on the wrong door."

"I see," I said. "So you intend to get the gentleman up here to attempt to identify me?"

"I don't think that will be necessary. I think we can I.D. you just from the description."

"Thanks a lot."

"The thing is, Mr. Phillips lists the time of the incident as approximately 1 o'clock."

"He could be mistaken."

"He could."

"Or it could be some *other* dumb-ass honky motherfucker."

"It could. I don't think the idea merits serious consideration."

"Perhaps not."

MacAullif looked at me. "Well, do you have any explanation?"

"All I can say is, the gentleman must be mistaken. I

thought this wasn't an interrogation and you didn't want to hear any of my lies."

MacAullif held up his hands. "It isn't, and I don't. Sorry. Let's move on."

"To what?"

MacAullif didn't answer me directly. He looked at me, frowned, then chuckled softly. "I should explain something to you," he said. "About homicide investigations. Since you obviously know nothing about them." MacAullif held up one finger. "Now, the murder of a pimp in Harlem, under normal circumstances, wouldn't rate this much attention. Know what standard procedure is? No, of course you don't. Well, it's forty-eight hours. That's how long we'd spend on this case. If we hadn't cracked it by then, it's go in the Unsolved Crimes file, and it never would get solved. Not unless we busted some punk for something else, and when we broke him he copped to this one too.

"So why is this case different? Two reasons. One is you. Your being on the scene. I recognized you the moment I saw you, of course. But I didn't let on. I kept it to myself 'cause I wanted to do some checking first. But right then and there, the minute I saw you, I made up my mind this was one we wouldn't just write off. You know what I mean?"

I did, but I didn't want to. What I wouldn't have given for MacAullif to put the case in the Unsolved Crimes File.

"I'm honored," I told him. "What's the other reason?"

"The witness."

"The witness?"

"Oh yeah, there's a witness." MacAullif seemed pleased. "You didn't know there was a witness? Good.

I'm glad the police are keeping ahead of you in some areas. Yeah, there's a witness. Which means I can justify keeping the investigation open. Without even using you as the reason."

"Who's the witness?"

"The witness is a young woman by the name of Celia Brown. She lives on the second floor of Darryl Jackson's building. Yesterday afternoon, from about 12:00 on, she was seated on the front steps of her building, waiting for a friend to arrive."

"That makes her a witness?"

"As to who entered the building, yes. Now, the times I'm going to give you are approximate, because she didn't really know. But we patched them together pretty well, and I would think they were fairly accurate."

MacAullif pulled another paper from the file. "About 12:10 a young woman arrived. White, 20's, dark hair, pretty. Best description we can get."

I realized MacAullif was watching me for a reaction. I didn't want to give him one, which was hard, seeing as how I knew someone that description would fit.

"Not much to go on," I said, casually.

"No, but it's a start. Now, here's where we get into the area of approximations. This Celia Brown had a walkman on. She was listening to music, or what passes for music these days."

"So."

"So it gives us a bit of a time frame. Celia figures the woman was up there for about three or four songs before she saw her come down again. So we figure three to four minutes a song, plus commercials, and we're talking fifteen to twenty minutes the woman was up there. So we figure she was downstairs 12:25, 12:30."

I shook my head. "Jesus Christ."

"I know, it's not accurate, but it's something. Particularly with what happened next."

"What's that."

"As soon as the woman left, a man came in. Not like they crossed on the stairs, or anything, but right after. Or, the way Celia Brown puts it, the same song was playing when the woman left as when the man came in." MacAullif raised his index finger. "It was still playing when the man came down. He went up, came right back down. That's significant. Now again, the description leaves a lot to be desired. He was white. She thinks he was young, and she thinks he was well-dressed. I say thinks because she couldn't really tell. See, the guy was wearing a full-length gray down parka with a hood. The hood was up and shielded most of his face. Celia Brown thinks there was something furtive about him. That's not the way she expressed it, but that's the general idea. I think she got the idea from the hood on the parka. She couldn't see his face, and she had the feeling he was trying to *keep* her from seeing his face, if you know what I mean. At any rate, he was right up and down."

MacAullif studied my face for a moment, then glanced at the sheet. "About two songs later someone else showed up. Another man. Also white. Older. Distinguished. Gray hair. Suit. He was up there a long time. We don't know when he left, but he was still there when Celia Brown's friend showed up about ten of one.

"So there's your time table. Young woman, in at 12:10, out at 12:25, 12:30. Young man, immediately thereafter, right up and down. Distinguished gentleman, up at 12:35, still there at ten of one." He looked at me. "What do you make of that?"

"Well," I said. "It's rather extraordinary, isn't it?"

"What do you mean?"

"That a disinterested witness should come forward and give you that detailed and specific information."

MacAullif nodded. "It most certainly is. You have put your finger right on it. I mean with the word, "disinterested." For your information, Celia Brown happens to be a junkie. The friend she was waiting for so impatiently happens to have been her connection. This, of course, is not the way she tells the story, but it's something we can infer. It also happens that Celia Brown has two counts of possession of narcotics pending."

"I see."

"She approached the public defender, who approached us, offering to plea-bargain the info for dropping the two counts of possession."

"Did you?"

"We certainly did. This is a murder case. We need all the help we can get. Besides, if we really want to get Celia Brown on possession of narcotics, we can pick her up again next week, it's no big deal."

"Won't all that rather impair her testimony if she happens to identify one of those people?"

"Her testimony ain't worth a damn. But we weren't buying testimony, we were buying information. However, if the fingerprints of the person she identifies happen to be on the knife, that's a different case altogether."

"Fingerprints?"

"Yeah. Didn't I mention the fingerprints?"

"No, you did not."

"Ah, well, we got fingerprints from the knife."

"You're kidding."

"No, I'm not. We got 'em. Most of 'em are too

smudged to do any good, but at least two of 'em are clear enough to I.D. Now it will probably turn out that the murderer wore gloves, and those fingerprints are from a couple of weeks before when someone was carving a roast, but there you are. On the other hand, if those fingerprints should independently match up with someone Celia Brown happens to I.D., Bingo!

"Anyway, let's get back to Celia Brown's schedule. The Skirt, the Parka, the Gray Hair.

"Scenario number one: the Skirt goes in there, talks to him for twenty minutes, has an argument, kills him and gets out; Parka goes in, knocks on the door, gets no answer and leaves, or finds him dead and leaves; Gray Hair arrives, finds him dead, and ransacks the apartment.

"Scenario number two: Skirt goes in, talks to him twenty minutes, leaves; Parka goes in, angry that Skirt's been there, kills him, and leaves; Gray Hair arrives and ransacks apartment.

"Scenario number three: Skirt arrives, talks, leaves; Parka arrives, goes to door, gets cold feet, turns around, leaves; Gray Hair arrives, kills gentleman, ransacks apartment."

He looked at me. "What do you think?"

"They all sound good to me," I said.

"Scenario number four: Skirt arrives, talks, leaves: Parka arrives, gets cold feet, leaves; Gray Hair arrives, talks, leaves; douche-bag private investigator arrives, kills him, trashes apartment, arranges elaborate coverup."

"That sounds a little farfetched to me."

"Perhaps. I could introduce you to five or six guys on the force to whom it doesn't."

"Great. So where does that leave us?"

"That leaves us with a nice, unsolved murder. Which happens to be my least favorite kind."

"So what do we do now?"

"We solve it." MacAullif pulled another paper from the file. "Let's take the victim, Darryl Jackson. Twenty-nine years of age. Eleven priors dating back about eight years. Mostly procurement—pimping to you. One aggravated assault—he beat up one of his hookers. One possession of grass. Nuisance busts, mostly. Not much to go on. But it does paint a picture of a not-too affluent pimp running a bunch of street hookers and taking the usual amount of heat for it."

MacAullif raised his finger. "Now, here's the interesting thing. These busts were all prior to about two years ago. Up till then he was getting knocked down pretty regular. But after that nothing."

I looked at him. "Are you telling me there was a payoff?"

He winced. "No, for Christ's sake. Jesus, why is it, you fucking civilians, every chance you get you yell police corruption? No, that's not what I mean. What I mean is, Darryl Jackson obviously moved on to something else."

"Such as?"

"I thought you were smart. What the hell would a pimp running a bunch of hookers naturally fall into?"

"Blackmail?"

"Good. But you get no points cause I had to give you a hint."

"You have evidence?"

"No. I don't have a thing. It's just what I think. It's logical. It's what would happen. The guy pimps around for years, and then one day he recognizes some john who's prominent enough he can't let his name get involved with a hooker. And there you are. Darryl Jackson retires, so to speak. He bleeds the guy white, and sets himself up in a slightly elevated business."

"What business?"

"Call girls. That may sound like the same thing, but it's not. There's a big difference between a street hooker and a high-priced call girl. And, of course, the opportunities for blackmail would naturally increase."

I couldn't help thinking about the video tapes. I tried to keep my face from showing it. "I see," I said.

"Now," MacAullif went on, "we've been trying to get a line on Darryl Jackson, and guess what? Nobody knows nothin'. Zip. We pulled in every street hooker used to work for him, and every one said the same thing—hadn't seen him in years. Now, they'd say that anyway, whether they knew it was a murder or not, but the thing is, I talked to them myself, and I believe 'em. I can tell the difference, you know. I can tell when somebody's telling the truth. Just like I can tell that you're not. But let that go, I said we weren't going to talk about that. Where was I? Oh yeah. Anyway, we can't get a line on the guy for the last two years. It's a blank. The hookers don't know, the people in his building don't know. No one knows. So whatever he was doing, he probably wasn't doing it in his building. So the way I figure it, he probably had a high-price call girl operation somewhere downtown. How do you figure it?"

The way I figured it, MacAullif was dangerous as bloody fucking hell. "You're the expert," I told him. "I hadn't really given it that much thought."

"I'll bet you hadn't," MacAullif said.

My beeper went off. With the direction the conversation had been going in, it was actually a welcome interruption.

MacAullif passed the phone over his desk. "Dial 9," he said. "Sometimes it works, sometimes it doesn't."

I dialed 9 and got an outside line. I called the office and got Wendy/Cheryl, who had a case for me to sign up that afternoon out in Queens. While I was writing it down my beeper went off again. This time, instead of "beep, beep, beep" it made a steady tone. That was my wife beeping me to call home.

I finished with Wendy/Cheryl, apologized to Mac-Aullif, dialed 9 again, and called my wife.

She had beeped me to remind me it was my turn to pick up the kids after school for the car pool in case I'd forgotten. I certainly had. I checked my watch. It was going to be close.

"I'm sorry," I told MacAullif, as I hung up. "I gotta run. I gotta pick up my kid at school."

"Oh yeah," he said. "And what was the other call?"

"Then I gotta run out and see a client in Queens."

He shrugged. "O.K. You can go. We were about finished here anyway."

"Good," I said. I started for the door.

"Just one thing," he said.

I stopped. "Yeah."

"You mind if I give you a piece of advice?"

I did mind, but I wasn't going to say so. "No."

He shrugged. "It's none of my business," he said, "but before you go out to Queens—if I were you, I'd sure as hell check the address."

18

IT WAS THE NEXT MORNING before I got to look at the tapes. It killed me to wait that long, particularly after what MacAullif had told me, but that's just the way things worked out.

After I left MacAullif's, I caught the subway uptown, picked up my car, and beat it over to East 84th Street just in time to pick up the kids. Pamela looked a bit strained when I dropped Joshua off, but then, I would have expected her to. I couldn't say anything to her in front of the kids, but I wasn't sure there was anything I wanted to tell her anyway. So I just dropped Joshua off and split.

Alice looked just as strained when I dropped Tommie off. I wasn't really looking forward to talking to her either, so I was kind of glad I had an assignment to go to. On the other hand, if I *hadn't*, I'd have pretended I had so I could go watch the tapes. So I guess the assignment wasn't that much of a blessing, after all.

On my way out to Queens they beeped me again, right off the fucking Grand Central, and by the time I wasted a half hour finding a phone, I was late for my appointment. I was also late for my appointment out in

West Hempstead, which was what they'd beeped me to give me.

At any rate, by the time I finished both assignments, it was too late to go to the office to look at the tapes. Or at least, there was no way of doing it without tipping Alice off to the fact I had them, and I wasn't ready to do that yet.

There was another reason I didn't want to go to the office: MacAullif. MacAullif was smart. Too smart. And I realized I couldn't trust him. Now maybe everything he told me was true. And maybe the *reason* he gave me for telling me was true.

But maybe not. Maybe it was a trap. Maybe he gave me all that information, because he thought some of it might mean something to me, and he wanted to find out what. Maybe he told me all that because he wanted to see what it would make me do.

Maybe he was having me watched.

That was the thought that haunted me all the way out to Queens and West Hempstead and back. And that was the thought that kept me from my office. Because it wouldn't be normal for me to go to my office at that time of night, and if MacAullif were having me watched, and I did anything out of the ordinary, it just might give him ideas.

I've never been followed, so I don't know the approved routine for spotting a shadow, but I tried. And I couldn't spot a thing. By the time I got back from West Hempstead, I was convinced of one of two things: either I wasn't being followed, or whoever was doing it was damn good.

At any rate, I didn't go to the office till the next morning, which was what I would have normally done in the course of my business, so there was no way it could possibly tip off anyone to anything.

I thanked my lucky stars I'd already rented the video player and bought the TV, cause that would have been a dead giveaway in case anyone was watching.

I closed the office door behind me and double-locked it. I picked up the mail, saw it was mostly bills, and threw it on the desk. I checked the answering machine for messages—there were none. Good.

I opened my desk drawer and pulled out the bag of video tapes. I took the video tapes out of the bag, set aside the one with Pamela's stellar performance on it, and surveyed the other five. They were identical. Nothing to choose from. Pick a tape, any tape. I did, and loaded it into the machine.

I turned the volume of the TV off, just in case anyone happened to be lurking outside in the hall. I suppose that was excessively paranoid, but I didn't really need sound anyway. I mean, when you've heard one grunt of passion, you've heard 'em all.

I put the machine on play. There was a burst of static, and then the tape flickered into view.

I could tell at once that this tape was different. This time production values were poor. The picture was dim, indicating the tape had been shot with existing light. And the camera appeared to be fixed, stationary.

The view was of a hotel room, and, more particularly, a hotel room bed. The camera seemed to be positioned above the head of the bed and slightly to one side, so that it was shooting diagonally down across the bed.

At the end of the bed, a girl was undressing. The girl was not Pamela. She was a white girl with blond hair, probably somewhere in her late twenties. A few seconds of watching her undress confirmed the fact that the tape had been shot with a stationary camera. It was only when she bent down to remove an article of clothing that I could see her face. Every time she straightened up, her head went out of frame. No cameraman alive would have ever shot it that way.

The girl finished undressing and got onto the bed. She was joined immediately by a gentleman who had obviously been undressing at the same time slightly out of frame. He appeared to be about thirty-five or forty. He also appeared to be somewhat of a nerd. He seemed to be pretty embarrassed about what he was doing. He also didn't seem to be particularly good at it. And even with the bad angle and the lousy lighting, I could tell that the girl was thoroughly bored with him.

I stopped the tape.

All right, now what have I got? I've got a picture of another hooker and a picture of a john. The fact that there was no lighting and the camera was fixed indicated that this was a setup, and the john knew nothing about it. Obviously, this was part of Darryl Jackson's blackmail setup. So the nerd could be one of his victims.

But so what? What did it do for me?

The answer was nothing. I didn't know who this guy was, and I had no way of finding out. On the other hand, unless he was the Parka, which seemed unlikely, I didn't *care* who he was.

I sped through the rest of the nerd's less than scintillating performance. Finally the picture dissolved the way it does when you turn the recorder off and then start recording again.

The picture cleared up, and Act II of my drama unfolded. Same set. Different cast. Definitely the same theme.

I sped through the rest of the tape, slowing down only long enough to identify the supporting players. There wasn't much to identify. I counted half a dozen girls, one of whom was Pamela, who appeared in two of the segments. I wondered if she was aware she was being filmed. She didn't appear to be, and I thought not. There'd be no reason for a blackmailing pimp to let the hookers in on his racket.

None of the other girls meant anything to me. Any of them might have been Jane, but I had no way of knowing.

I also counted thirteen johns, all different. No repeat performances. But why would there be? I guess once is enough for blackmail. I mean it's not like you were gonna edit the shit, and wanted to get a good performance. As long as the guy's face showed, he was dead meat.

None of the guys meant anything to me. I guess four or five of 'em could have been Parka, but I had no way of telling. Two of 'em might have been Gray Hair, but I doubted it. One looked flabby, and one looked dumb. Looking at 'em, the word distinguished didn't really ring a bell.

I rewound the tape and took it out of the machine. I took a piece of masking tape, stuck it on the cassette, and marked it #1, so I could tell it from the other ones.

I took out another tape and was about to stick it in the machine when my beeper went off. I muttered some remark or other about Richard's parentage, shut off my beeper, and called the office.

Wendy/Cheryl had a new case for me. Some guy on West 94th Street had fallen down in McDonald's and broken his wrist. I told her I'd take it and hung up the phone.

I didn't really want to take the case, but then I figured if MacAullif was really watching me, I ought to let him see that I was just acting normal. So I called up the client and told him I'd be right over.

I grabbed my briefcase, ran out, hopped a subway uptown, and signed up the client. It was a record sign-up, even for me. I never even took off my coat. I signed him up, snapped his picture, and was on my way out the door, before the poor son of a bitch even knew what hit him.

I took the subway back downtown, went back to the office, and cued up tape #2.

It was very like tape #1, except that this time Pamela Berringer appeared in three of the segments. For my money, she was the class act of the lot, but then I guess a detective is always prejudiced in favor of his own client.

I was halfway through tape #3 when I found it. Holy shit! I pushed the button, froze the frame.

Even naked, the gentleman in the picture looked distinguished. Every gray hair was neatly trimmed, and perfectly in place. He had a manicured look about him, a plastic look you normally associate with a soap opera star.

But the thing was, I knew him. I'd seen him before. I had no idea where, but I knew I had seen that face.

What makes this remarkable is the fact that I am no better with faces than I am with names. My wife and I will be watching television and she'll suddenly grab my arm and say, "Do you know who that is?" And I won't. Even though I'll have seen him in something else, and know perfectly well who it is when she tells me the name, I won't be able to place the guy. It's partially because I have trouble transposing people from one setting to another. What I mean is, if I see the father of one of Tommie's classmates at school, I'll recognize him as so-and-so's father, but if I run into the same guy in the supermarket, I'll be thinking to myself, "Who is this guy?"

All the same, I had seen Gray Hair before. And I was pretty sure he wasn't someone I'd ever met. And I was pretty sure he wasn't someone I'd seen on TV. Which didn't leave many options. I must have seen his picture somewhere.

I ejected the tape and switched off the machine. I labeled the tape #3 and put it back in its box. I switched off the VCR and the TV. I put on my coat and went out.

I walked down to the New York Public Library on 42nd Street and Fifth Avenue. I went up to the periodical room, waited in line, and asked for back copies of the New York *Post*. The guy at the counter wanted to know what issues. I didn't know. I had no idea when I'd seen the picture, so one issue was as good as another. I decided to work backwards. I asked for the whole last week.

It turned out you could only get two papers at a time. And you had to fill out a form to get them. I filled out the form, wrote out a request for the last two days, handed it in, and the guy gave me the two papers. I took them over to one of the tables and began going through them.

On the one hand, it was fast because all I had to do was scan for pictures. But on the other, it was slow, because every two issues I had to fill out another damn request from and wait in line again. I'd filled out ten forms and scanned through twenty issues when I realized I wasn't really accomplishing anything other than giving myself a headache.

I stopped and thought a bit, something I should have done to begin with.

Gray Hair wasn't an actor or TV personality, but he was a prominent enough person to have gotten his picture in the paper often enough that I had seen it. And he was prominent enough that he couldn't afford a scandal, and was thus a likely target for blackmail. Which meant he was either a very influential businessman, or a politician. If he was a businessman, it didn't do me any good, because I couldn't think of any common link that would be helpful. But if he was a politician, there was something all politicians had in common. They had to get elected.

I filled out another form, this time asking for two issues from November of last year.

Four forms and seven issues later, I found it. There he was, Congressman Charles C. Blaine, running for reelection. He looked a little different with his clothes on, but it was Gray Hair, all right.

I had just made the connection when I spotted him. I can't give myself any credit for doing so. I guess it was just that I felt so good when I made the I.D., that I looked up in exultation, and the guy at the end of the table ducked back into his book.

If he hadn't, I wouldn't have spotted him. His head was up and he was looking off into space, as if reflecting on something he was reading. He must have been watching me with peripheral vision, and I never would have noticed him, particularly excited as I was at having identified the congressman. But when my head jerked up, his jerked down, and I caught the movement out of the corner of my eye.

That sobered me right up. MacAullif, you son of a bitch.

I must admit I was scared shitless. I immediately bent my head back down and began scanning through the paper again. This was for two reasons: one, to give me time to think; two, so my friend wouldn't think I'd found what I was looking for.

Thank god I hadn't done what I'd been about to do, which was whip out my notebook and write down the name, Charles C. Blaine. Bad as I am with names, this was one I would have to remember. I said it over to myself a few times as I turned the pages of the paper.

I finished the paper, went back to the counter, filled in a form, and took out two papers from July two years back. I took 'em back to my table and poured through them.

I filed out five more slips for various months of various years. By then I figured I'd thrown up as much of a smoke screen as I could. Either it had worked or it hadn't. I just had to hope.

The whole time, of course, I was sizing up my tail. He was young, say mid-twenties. He had sandy hair and glasses, and looked just like a college student doing research for a mid-term, but I knew he wasn't. I dubbed him 'Sandy,' and started trying to figure out what to do about him.

Sandy was going to be a problem. Having gotten the

hot lead on the Congressman, naturally I wanted to follow up on it. But, of course, I didn't want MacAullif to
know I was doing it. And it wasn't just that I didn't
want to give him the lead to the Congressman. It was
that I didn't want to do anything that would confirm his
suspicion that I was mixed up in this thing. My going
through the newspapers wouldn't have done it—he
couldn't be sure I wasn't just doing research for
Richard. But going to the Congressman would be something else. There was no way MacAullif was gonna
believe Congressman Charles C. Blaine had engaged
Richard's services. Going there would be a dead
giveaway.

So what was I gonna do about Sandy? The answer
was incredibly simple, and at the same time incredibly
hard: I was gonna have to ditch him.

I've never ditched a shadow before. I'm sure there
are prescribed methods for doing it, but I didn't know
'em. And the thing was, I not only wanted to ditch him,
I wanted to ditch him so he wouldn't realize he'd been
ditched. So MacAullif wouldn't know I'd spotted the
shadow. So MacAullif wouldn't know I was wise. So I
could go on playing the innocent, dumb, bumbling
boob, which, aside from the innocent part, wasn't too
hard for me.

I didn't know how to do it, and the more I thought
about it the less I came up with. I decided to stop thinking and just do something. Set the wheels in motion and
see what transpired.

So I took the last batch of papers back to the counter,
didn't sign out any more, went back to the table, and
put on my coat.

Oddly enough, Sandy seemed to have finished his
research too. Out of the corner of my eye I saw him

gathering up his books. I ignored him and headed for the door.

I walked over to Times Square and went down in the subway. I bought a token, went through the turnstile, and went down the steps to the Broadway uptown platform, as if I were on my way home.

I walked halfway down the platform, as I always do to get the right car to line up with the exit at the 103rd Street station. I stopped and leaned against a column. Damned if Sandy wasn't taking the same train. He was standing four columns down the platform, reading a book. Always the diligent student.

The local pulled into the station. The doors opened, and the passengers poured out.

I went in the doors on the uptown end of a car. Sandy got in the same car, through the center doors.

The car was full enough that there were no seats, so there was nothing strange about me sliding back the door at the end of the car, and going through into the next car.

As I came through the door into the next car, I reached under my coat and switched on my beeper. "Beep, beep, beep," echoed through the car. I threw up my hands in disgust, and stepped off the train onto the platform, just as the door closed.

I switched off my beeper, pulled out my notebook, and stepped up to the pay phone on a pillar on the platform. I was standing there pretending to make a call when the train pulled out of the station. I could see Sandy watching out the window in helpless frustration as he went by.

Having sent Sandy uptown on the IRT, I walked across the station, and caught the BMT downtown. It always pays to be careful.

19

I'VE NEVER CALLED on a congressman before. Apparently, it isn't easy. When I got there, there were about a dozen people seated in the outer office waiting to get in. From the looks on their faces, a lot of them had been waiting for some time.

I walked up to the receptionist at the desk.

"May I help you?" she asked.

"Yes," I said. "I'd like to see Congressman Blaine."

She smiled slightly. "Do you have an appointment?"

"No, I don't," I told her.

"Then I'm afraid it won't be possible. The Congressman sees people only by appointment."

"My business is rather urgent."

She smiled slightly again. "Our constituents' business is always urgent." She gestured to the people in the room. "These people also have urgent business. And they have appointments."

"I understand that," I said. "But I think the Congressman will still want to see me. Could you at least inform him that I'm here?"

She was getting a little annoyed at my persistence. I got the impression that she was one of those people who enjoy being able to say no.

"Very well," she said icily. "Your name, sir?"

"Darryl Jackson."

"Just a minute, Mr. Jackson," she said.

She got up from the desk and went to the door to the inner office. She edged her way through the door, as if not wanting to give anyone a glimpse into the office beyond.

When she emerged a minute later there was a marked change in her demeanor.

"Could you tell me the nature of your business, Mr. Jackson?"

"I prefer to discuss it with the Congressman."

"I understand. But, just generally, what is it you wish to discuss?"

"Publicity."

She digested the information and disappeared once again behind the door.

I went over and sat down with the other constituents.

I needn't have bothered. She was back in a minute. She stopped in the doorway with her hand on the knob.

"Mr. Jackson," she said.

I got up and walked to the door with the eyes of everyone in the room on me. I have never felt so hated in my life. I nodded shortly to the receptionist, and went in the door.

Congressman Charles C. Blaine looked like he did in his photos, only more so. I swear the guy must have worn makeup. I mean, a fifty-year-old man can't *have* a complexion like that. And you would have thought he must have had a barber hiding in the next room, shaving him every half hour. No stubble. Not even a hair.

He had a look of frosty reserve one normally associated with bankers. I wondered if this was his customary face for receiving constituents, or if he had just put it on for me.

He stood up when I came in. He was watching me closely, as if trying to figure out if he had ever seen me before. I could have told him he hadn't. He came around his desk and shook my hand.

"Darryl Jackson?" he said.

"Congressman Blaine?"

He indicated a chair in front of his desk. "Please sit down."

I sat. He retreated behind his desk and sat down too.

"Now, what can I do for you?" he said.

"Well, to begin with," I said, "I should clarify something. I'm not Darryl Jackson. I'm Darryl Jackson's representative. Darryl Jackson couldn't be with us today, largely due to the fact that someone stuck a carving knife in his back."

I was looking at him for a reaction, but he wasn't giving me one. I guess you didn't get to be a congressman by letting people know what you were thinking.

"Perhaps you heard about it," I said. I shrugged. "Perhaps not. In any event, I bet you're sitting there thinking to yourself, how bad is this gonna be? Well, not so bad. The publicity I want to talk to you about is the publicity you don't want. I'm a private detective and I'm investigating the Darryl Jackson murder. I may be in the position to do you a service. If I can, I would expect to be paid.

"But we can discuss that later. Right now, I'd like to ask you a few questions. To begin with, does the name Darryl Jackson mean anything to you?"

"No."

"That's funny, since it got me in here to see you. But I'll let that go. For your information, Darryl Jackson was killed the day before yesterday sometime between 12:00 and 1:00 in the afternoon. It might be wise for you to start considering what you were doing long about then."

"I don't see why, since I don't know any Darryl Jackson."

"Of course. Well, for your information, he was a pimp and a blackmailer. He lived at 307 West 127th Street. That's where he was killed, by the way. Now, the police have a witness who saw you going into that building about that time. So if you killed him, it's just too bad, cause they're gonna get you. And if you *didn't* kill him, it's worse, cause they're probably gonna get you anyway. At any rate, all I'm saying is, when you searched the apartment, I hope you were smart enough to wear gloves."

"I don't know what you're talking about."

"Of course not. I don't either. I'm just talking. If I say anything that rings a bell, let me know."

Congressman Blaine stood up. "You've said enough. Now get out."

"That's not the bell I was hoping for," I said. I stood up too.

"I'm afraid it's the one you rang," he said. He gestured with his arm. "There's the door."

"I see it," I said. "I hope I can quote you on this. You don't know Darryl Jackson. You are not involved with any of Darryl Jackson's hookers. You were not paying him blackmail. And you were not in his apartment on the afternoon in question."

I started for the door.

His voice rang out. It was an eloquent voice, a speaker's voice. "Just a minute," it said.

I stopped. "Yes?"

"What do you mean, 'quote'?"

"Quote. You know, quote. As in repeat what someone said. Like if I'm talking to the newspapers and they ask me about the crime, I can say, well now, Congressman Blaine denied all knowledge of it."

His eyes were hard. "You're going to the newspapers?"

"Certainly not," I said. "I told you before, I was talking about publicity. This is the type of publicity I'm talking about. It's the type that I want to control, and the type that I'm sure you want to control. Now, as I said, I'm in a position where I may be able to do you a service. If I can, I will expect some compensation. Now, you relax, take it easy, have a good day. You've got twelve constituents waiting out there to see you, and I wouldn't want to keep 'em waiting. It's been very nice talking to you, and I promise you I will call on you again."

I bowed and smiled my way out the door. In the waiting room I smiled at the receptionist, said, "Thank you very much. I believe the Congressman is free now," turned, and walked out the door.

Outside, I assessed the situation. Not bad. I'd gotten a nibble. A small rise out of him. Basically, all the confirmation that I needed. And I'd only dropped a few hints. Nothing conclusive. Nothing that *definitely* constituted blackmail. And I'd left the door open for future conversations. I'd stirred him up a bit. Given him something to stew about. It would be interesting to hear what he said when I called on him again.

20

"THE COPS have a witness."

"What?"

I was sitting with Pamela Berringer in a small cafe on Broadway. After leaving the Congressman, I'd called her and told her to meet me there 'cause I needed to talk with her. I figured it might be the last chance I'd get. Naturally, I didn't want MacAullif to get a lead to her, and I couldn't count on ditching my shadow again. So while Sandy was playing tag on the subways seemed like a good time.

She didn't want to come—she wasn't involved, she saw no point, she had nothing to say—but she came.

Her coat was over the back of her chair. She had on a pink sweater. She looked young, frightened, helpless.

Virginal.

"The cops have a witness in the Darryl Jackson murder."

She looked at me. "Are you kidding?"

"No. I know you appreciate my sense of humor, but I rarely kid about murders, particularly ones involving

157

me. The cops have a witness. A young, black girl with a walkman on. She was sitting on the steps of that building. She saw who went in and out."

Pamela tensed. "And?"

"And what?" I said. "If you weren't there, she couldn't have seen you."

She bit her lip. "That's right."

"Well, were you there or not?"

"No. I wasn't."

"Then what I'm going to tell you will probably be of no interest to you, but I'm gonna tell you anyway. According to this girl, about 12:10 a young woman went in. White, twenties, pretty. Sound like anyone you know?"

"No. It could be anyone."

"It could, but I think it was you."

"Well, it wasn't."

"You don't lie very well. You ought to practice, if you expect to keep on fooling dear old Ronnie. I'm not so sure you are, anyway. It happens that after this young woman who wasn't you left, a young man answering Ronnie's description who'd been waiting around outside went in right behind her."

"My god."

"Of course, if it wasn't you, it wasn't him, so you got nothing to worry about."

"What did he do?"

"This guy who wasn't Ronnie? He went right in and right back out again."

"Oh."

"The cops figure either he knocked on the door and got no answer cause the guy was dead, or he got cold feet and never even knocked, or he went in and found the body, or he went in and killed him."

She stared at me. "How do you know all that?"

"I'm a detective."

I loved saying that. It was such a jive thing to say. But she accepted it. She took it for an answer.

"Oh," she said.

I was staring right at her, and her eyes faltered. She looked down at her plate.

While I had her off balance, I shot at her, "Does Ronnie have a gray parka?"

She looked up startled. "What?"

"Ronnie. Your husband. Does he own a gray parka?"

"Yes. Why?"

"That's what the young man was wearing."

Pamela said nothing. She looked miserable.

"Of course, it wasn't you, so it wasn't him. Which is fortunate. You sure it wasn't you?"

"No, no," she said weakly, tonelessly. "It wasn't me." She took a breath, seemed to pull herself together. "Look, it wasn't me, but I'm still in terrible trouble. My fingerprints are in that apartment. If the cops find that tape, I'm dead."

"That's what I've been trying to tell you. That's why I suggested it would be a very good idea if you could come up with some sort of alibi for the hours from 12:00 to 1:00. As I recall, you didn't take kindly to the suggestion."

"Because I don't *have* one," she said. "Don't you understand?"

"Yeah. I'm afraid I do."

She leaned across the table. "Look. Please. I'm going crazy. You gotta help me. You're very smart and very resourceful. You must be, to have all that information. You gotta do something for me. You gotta find out if the police have that tape."

I couldn't do it to her anymore. She was just too distraught.

"They don't," I told her.

She stared at me, open-mouthed. "What?"

"I have the tape."

She was astounded. "You what? You have? But— How did you get it?"

"That doesn't matter. The important thing is, I have it, and the police aren't going to find it. So you can stop worrying."

"Give it to me."

"I don't have it with me."

"Let's go get it."

"No."

She looked at me. "No? What do you mean, no? I asked you to get that tape. That's what this was all about. You said you'd try to get it for me."

"I know I did. But things have changed. Now it's murder. That tape may be the only thing standing between me and a murder rap."

"But you couldn't—"

"I won't. I'm not going to let the police have it. I'm not going to let anyone see it. But I'm not giving it up, either. Not now, anyway. Not till this thing is settled. Now, I promise you, I'll protect your reputation if I can, but I'm not going to jail for you."

She looked at me. "You've seen the tape."

"Yes."

"I know you have. Your manner's changed. Just the inflection you used when you said, 'protect your reputation'. The trace of irony. The slightly mocking tone."

I looked at her. "Hey, what are you saying?"

"You've judged me."

"What?"

"You've judged me. Haven't you? Before you were willing to give me the benefit of the doubt. Now you've made up your mind."

I was having trouble meeting her eyes. "I don't know what you mean."

"Oh, yes you do. You saw the tape. And it changed you. You can't forgive me anymore. Can you?"

That was too much. She'd pushed too hard. I'd done a lot for this ingrate, and I wasn't going to let her browbeat me.

"All right," I said. "That's enough. You wanna talk about the benefit of the doubt? I've given you the benefit of the doubt. I've taken you on faith. You wanna know the faith I've taken you on? I've put my ass on the line believing in a girl who didn't know what an escort service was."

Her eyes faltered slightly. "I see. But you never raised the point until you saw that tape."

I said nothing. I sat and waited.

"All right," she said. "If it makes such a difference. All right, let's say for the sake of argument, I knew there might be more involved than just going to dinner. And I still went." She looked in my eyes, pleadingly. "But you must believe me. When I got there, I couldn't do it. I swear to you. I couldn't do it. That man raped me. He *did*. No matter why I went there, or how I went there, what happened happened. And what happened was I was beaten and raped. And that's the truth."

"O.K.," I said.

She looked at me closely. "You say 'O.K.', but you don't mean it. Because of the tape. And not because of *what* I did on the tape. Because of *how* I did it."

She paused. Looked down. Took a breath. Then she looked up at me. She was no longer the timid little girl. Nor was she embarrassed any more. She was strong now, and in complete control.

"I was forced to make that tape. And everything else I did. I was forced to do. I had no choice. So I did it. I didn't want to do it, but I did it. You don't understand that because you've never been in my position. You didn't know Darryl Jackson. You don't know what it's like to be threatened by someone like him. I'd have done anything he told me to. I didn't want to make that tape, but he told me to, so I did.

"And now you've seen that tape and it's changed you. And I know why."

She paused again. Then looked straight at me. "I was *good* at it. I didn't want to do those things, but when I was made to do them, there wasn't any tentativeness, any hesitation. That's what you can't forgive."

"That's not true," I said. But I couldn't meet her eyes.

"You know it's true." I was still looking down, but I could hear the scorn in her voice. "Let me ask you something Mr. Moral One, Mr. Morality. You saw the tape. What did you feel when you saw it? Cool and impartial? Just evidence to look at, right? Or did it turn you on? Did it get you hot, excited? And if it did—were you ashamed that it did? Or did you consider your reaction perfectly normal? Did you think, who *wouldn't* be turned on?"

Her eyes were blazing into me, and I couldn't meet 'em. I said nothing. There was nothing to say. She had me. Game, set, match to Pamela. She was right up and down the line.

21

MY WIFE GAVE ME HELL when I got home. I guess it just wasn't my day. First Pamela Berringer getting the better of me, and then my wife. I'd handled the men pretty well, Sandy and the Congressman, but women seemed to be my downfall. At any rate, Alice jumped on me the minute I got in the door.

"Pamela Berringer called," she said.

There is no way to do her justice in describing her tone of voice. Suffice to say, it was a flat accusation.

"Oh," I said neutrally, the snappiest response I could come up with under the circumstances.

"You have her tape," Alice said.

"Yes."

"You didn't tell her. You didn't tell me."

"I had my reasons."

"I'll bet."

There was a pause, and then:

"You saw it."

"What?"

"You saw the tape. You watched it."

163

"Of course I watched it. How else would I have known what it was?"

"I'll bet you watched the whole thing."

"Oh, come on now."

"Did you?"

"I skimmed it."

"I'll bet."

It went on like that for some time. Suffice to say, I wound up the greatest lecher since the dawn of time. My wife was adamant. Nothing I could say would shake her. It was kinda funny, really. My wife was ready to *defend* Pamela to the death for making the tape. But she was ready to *condemn* me to death for having watched it.

I learned a bitter truth that night. Morality is relative. It's not *what* people do.

It's who does it.

22

It snowed that night. A good twelve inches. Late November is early in Manhattan for snow, so we weren't prepared for it, especially since all the local TV forecasters had predicted heavy rain. In the morning they were all backtracking nimbly and talking about 'Arctic flows' and 'inverted high pressure systems' and a whole bunch of other gobbledegook, all of which added up to the fact that it was snowing. I could tell that just by looking out the window.

The snow closed the East Side Day School, which meant I didn't have to drive Tommie and Joshua, since it was my turn for the car pool. It also suspended alternate-side parking, which meant I didn't have to move my car, which had been on the bad side, of course, so I could get out for the school run. I didn't even bother digging it out. I left it buried under a ton of snow and took the subway down to the office.

There were no messages on the answering machine, but I had expected none. Snow creates a time lag in my business. No one wants to deal with a lawyer in the middle of a snowstorm, so the usual routine cases are put off till the next day. So today would be dead. Tomorrow would be crazy, however, as all the people who slipped on the ice and snow and went to the hospital today would start calling in.

I switched on my beeper just in case, however, and sat down to ponder my next move. I wasn't sure what it was. I had a few leads, a few clues, but that was it. The Congressman was almost certainly Gray Hair, but had he killed him? I didn't know. He might have, but so might Pamela, or even Ronnie baby. So how could I tell?

The problem was, figuring out who had committed murders was not really in my field of expertise. Getting camera angles on broken sidewalks so they looked like disaster areas was more in my line.

After some reflection, it occurred to me that there was one thing that I could still do. I could finish watching the tapes.

I threaded up tape #3, thinking what Alice would say if she knew I had *six* of the damn things. I hadn't rewound it, so it was right where I'd left it when I'd frozen it on the picture of Congressman Blaine. I realized I hadn't even watched the gentleman's performance. Perhaps it would be interesting to see how he served his constituents.

I switched the tape on. Once again, the Congressman's face filled the screen. As he moved into position, I saw what I hadn't realized before: his partner was Pamela.

After my talk with Pamela last night, I didn't really want to watch this.

But I did.

I don't know how to rate the Congressman's performance. I could damn it with faint praise: it was adequate. Actually, it was not bad.

But there was something else, too, and it bothered me. It really bothered me, and not just because it was with Pamela, although I'm sure that had something to do with it. It was the look on the Congressman's face. Aside from the ecstacy, of course, there was a look that was gloating, almost cruel. I'm sure I projected a lot of it because I didn't like the man, but I swear it was there.

I sped through most of it, and through the rest of the tape. I sped through the other tapes too. I learned nothing new, except for the fact that the Congressman appeared in segments on two of the other tapes. He was the only john who appeared more than once, a good indication that he was the big fish in the pond. In every case, his partner was Pamela, which indicated to me that at least he was a man of discernment.

I rewound all the tapes, put them back in the boxes, sat, and thought some more. The only thing I came up with was the fact that I was getting hungry.

I walked out to Broadway and got a slice of pizza. As I stood in the pizza parlor eating it, I spotted Sandy standing on the sidewalk outside. He was all bundled up in a heavy coat and hood, and he was turned sideways and trying to look inconspicuous, but it was Sandy all right.

I was glad to see him. His presence confirmed one thing: he hadn't realized I'd ditched him deliberately. If he had, he'd have reported to MacAullif that I was wise, and MacAullif would have pulled him off the job and assigned someone else. So the cops were still guessing.

I finished my pizza and walked down Broadway to a penny arcade. I went in and started playing Megazone,

one of the video games. Three quarters later, I noticed a guy playing Q-bert a few machines down the row. The guy had been in the pizza parlor with me. He was older than Sandy, and he looked a little like a college professor. It struck me kind of funny. Sandy, the poor student, had fucked up the assignment, and his teacher had come along with him this time to show him how to do it.

I left the penny arcade and led Sandy and the Professor back to my office.

I sat down and reassessed the situation. O.K. I was still in the clear. The cops weren't wise to the fact that I was wise to them. If they had been, they'd have pulled Sandy off the job. Instead they'd reinforced him with the Professor. So they regarded my ditching Sandy as an accident, and they were just taking care to make sure it didn't happen again.

And it probably wouldn't happen again. I'd walked away from one man, but I probably couldn't walk away from two, particularly when they'd been alerted to see it didn't happen.

So what the hell could I do? I thought about it, and the answer was: nothing. MacAullif had restricted my movements, so I couldn't do anything. 'Cause anything I did would tip him off to the fact I was involved, and I couldn't afford to do that.

Why not?

The thought chilled me. Why not? I was in an impossible position. As long as I operated on the premise that I couldn't do anything that would give MacAullif a lead, I was stymied. But suppose I threw that premise away? After all, MacAullif knew I was involved, or he wouldn't be wasting all the time and manpower on me.

So what if I confirmed his suspicions? What would that do to me? Or, as I always ask myself, how bad could it be?

I started thinking along those lines. So far I'd accomplished nothing because I'd been bending all my energies toward keeping MacAullif from getting a lead. Suppose I turned things around? Suppose I stirred things up a bit?

Suppose I *gave* him a lead?

23

THIS TIME I didn't bother with any formalities. I just walked straight through the crowded waiting room up to the receptionist's desk and said shortly, "Tell the Congressman I'm here."

Her reaction was encouraging. She regarded me as if I were a hitman sent by the Mafia. She got up, edged around the corner of her desk, and virtually fled into the inner office.

She was back in moments.

"Mr. Jackson," she said.

I went through the door. I swear she backed away from me as I did.

Congressman Blaine was all cordiality this time. He was up and around the desk with his hand extended before I was even halfway across the room.

"Come in, come in," he said, smiling and shaking hands. "Do sit down, Mr.—"

"Jackson will do," I said.

"Yes, but that's not your name, is it?"

"No."

The Congressman sat down. "Well, then, who are you?"

"That's not important," I told him.

He frowned slightly. "I like to know who I'm dealing with."

"That's all right. You're not dealing with me."

"True. But I might."

"Oh?"

"I believe you said you were a private detective. Sometimes in the course of my business it becomes necessary for me to employ one. You strike me as a very competent and resourceful man, and it is conceivable that at some time I might be able to offer you employment."

"I'll put it on my resume," I said.

He frowned. "What?"

"A tentative, potential, future job possibility is rather nebulous. But I'll certainly consider it."

"How would I contact you?"

"Don't worry. I'll contact you."

He frowned again. "This interview is not going exactly as planned. I would like to know your name."

"I gathered that."

"But you're not going to tell me?"

"No."

"Is there any reason why you don't want me to know who you are?"

I shrugged. "Not really. Is there any reason why you don't want to admit that you were in Darryl Jackson's apartment?"

"No. Because I wasn't."

"Of course. I was just wondering if you found the book."

"The book?"

"The address book. The book of johns. Or blackmail victims, if you prefer. Darryl Jackson must have had some book like that. But the police don't have it. So the way I see it, either the murderer took it, or you took it. Unless, of course, the two are one and the same."

He stared at me. "Do you realize you're accusing me of murder?"

"No, I hadn't. Thank you for pointing it out to me. But no, I was just exploring the possibilities. You're sure you don't know any Darryl Jackson?"

"Quite sure."

"That's a shame. Still, I might be able to do you a service. Actually, I've done you a service already, just keeping the police off your back."

The Congressman looked at me narrowly. "I see. And now you want to be paid?"

"Oh no," I said. "I've barely gotten started. I haven't even shown you the worth of my work. If I can really do something for you, when I've really accomplished something, then we can talk about compensation."

"I'm not asking you to do anything for me."

"I understand that. But a private detective has to play the game the way he sees it. Sometimes he has to act on his own initiative. And sometimes the things he does benefit certain people. And then, of course, he expects to be paid."

The Congressman said nothing. He was sizing me up the way a cat sizes up a mouse. I was glad I wasn't running for office against him.

"Well," I said. "That's all I came to say."

I stood up. So did he.

"And you won't tell me where I can reach you?" he said.

"No."

"And you won't tell me your name?"

"It would serve no purpose."

"I still want to know."

I looked at him. "It must be hard," I said, "to run for office, win, find oneself well fixed in a position of power, and still not be able to get what one wants."

24

I FELT PRETTY GOOD leaving the Congressman's office. Of course, it always feels good to do something you didn't think you wanted to do.

Yeah, this was more like it. I'd been too passive before. I'd been hanging back, biding my time, waiting for things to happen. Now I was making 'em happen. Stirring things up.

I wondered what MacAullif would make of the Congressman. It was a pleasant thought. I wondered if Sandy and the Professor had phoned in yet. I was sure they had. One of them would have stood guard on the office while the other ran out to phone.

I didn't look for them as I walked out into the street, but I knew they'd be there. Well, I didn't care. I was getting action. I was feeling good. Now, I thought, while I'm in the mood, who shall I fuck with next?

The obvious answer was Pamela. Up till now I'd been too soft on her—let her get away with telling me lies—largely because I felt sorry for her. Well, no more of that. It was time to come down on her hard.

Which presented a problem: Sandy and the Professor.

Cause if there was one thing I was not going to do, it was lead MacAullif to Pamela Berringer.

So how the hell could I swing it, assuming I could swing it at all? Well, certainly not the way I'd done it the first time. Not passing it off as an accident. If I managed to ditch 'em at all, they'd have to know they'd been ditched.

I thought along those lines. All right, if they're gonna know they've been ditched, then they have to know I spotted 'em. So the first thing to do was spot 'em.

I stopped and looked in the window of a store. After a minute or two I turned my head and saw Sandy standing in the doorway of a store down the street. I turned back to the window. After a few seconds, I turned and looked at him again, then turned quickly back. Then I moved away, and walked casually down the street.

O.K. Now they know I spotted 'em. Now what?

The problem was I didn't know. I was playing it by ear. Letting them know I'd spotted them was the easy part. But what did I do now?

A cab came down the street. On an impulse, I hailed it and got in, something I rarely do, taxi prices being what they are.

I glanced in the rear window and saw Sandy and the Professor piling into a cab behind.

The cabbie saw me looking out the window through his rearview mirror. He was a young guy, and looked like an out of work actor, which was something I knew something about.

"Hey," he said. "Are you being followed?"

"Sure looks that way," I told him. "Can you do anything about it?"

He shook his head. "Not in this snow, I can't."

Snow. It sounded like a cue. It occurred to me, if I were a detective in a movie, snow would suggest something to me.

It did.

"I don't suppose," I said, "you could engineer a skid?"

He turned around and looked at me. "A what?"

"A skid," I told him. "A skid in the snow. Slide your cab across the street and stop."

"Are you kidding me?"

"Not at all. It doesn't have to be artistic or anything. Just skid to a stop."

"Now?"

"No. I'll tell you when. Can you do it?"

"Give it a try."

"Be sure you block the whole street."

"That much I figured out."

We were going down a one-way street, which was good, 'cause it was narrow, and what with the snow and all, there was barely room for two cars to get by. We were coming up on a traffic light. Waiting at the light, was another cab with its light on.

"O.K.," I said. "Right behind that cab."

The cabbie accelerated slightly, hit the brakes, and fishtailed. He spun out diagonally across the street and came to a stop not twenty feet from the waiting cab.

I slapped a ten dollar bill in his hand.

"Don't be too quick about getting untangled," I said.

I opened the door and hopped out. I ran to the corner and hopped in the other cab. The light changed, and we took off.

Through the rear window I could see Sandy and the Professor standing helplessly in the street and hurling curses at the fishtailed cab.

25

I WANTED TO HAVE as many strings to my bow as possible before I confronted Pamela Berringer, so I decided to engineer a coincidence.

I knew from casual conversations with the Berringers during the course of the car pool that Ronnie worked for an insurance agency somewhere near the World Trade Center. I wasn't sure of the name of it—I'm terrible with names—but it seemed to me it was one of the presidents, possibly Monroe or Madison.

I took the cab to the World Trade Center, got out, and hunted up a pay phone.

The Madison Insurance Agency had never heard of Ron Berringer, but the Monroe Agency had. Had he been in, I was prepared to be conveniently disconnected before his secretary got him on the phone, but she told me he was out to lunch and was expected back around 2:00. She asked me if I wanted to leave a message, but I told her, no, I'd try back later.

I hung up the phone and checked my watch. 1:30. Perfect.

I called information again and got the address of the

Monroe Agency. I could have just asked the secretary, but I wanted to get off the phone before she asked me too many questions, seeing as how I didn't really have any answers.

The address of the agency was on John Street, not two blocks from where I was. I strolled over leisurely, stopping every now and then to see if anyone was taking any interest in me. No one was. All in all, it just wasn't Sandy and the Professor's day.

I stopped outside the building and took my camera out of my coat pocket. During the summer I carry my camera in my briefcase, but in the winter I just slide it into my coat pocket, which is much more convenient. See, a lot of the sign-ups I do are in hospitals, and a lot of hospitals won't let you walk in with a briefcase or a camera, because a lot of hospitals have restrictions about taking pictures. So all I can take in is just a sign-up kit and a clipboard. That's why my Canon Snappy 50 is perfect for my job. It's small and compact, and slides right into a coat pocket. In the summer, with no overcoat, in order to get into hospitals, I have to wear the damn thing around my neck and tucked under my armpit, but in the winter it's a breeze.

I'd forgotten to reload the camera after taking out the roll with the shots of the guy who'd fallen at McDonald's, which was great for me, since I didn't really want to take any pictures and I didn't want Richard giving me any grief about wasting any film.

I took the camera and started snapping shots of the sidewalk in front of Ronnie Berringer's office building. It was a good thing these weren't real Location of Accident pictures: first, because there was no film in the camera, and second, because even if there had been the shots wouldn't have been any good. There simply wasn't any defect. There was no snow on the sidewalk, no icy patch that could have caused a poor pedestrian to slip. It had been beautifully cleared. And the sidewalk itself was perfect. The concrete could have been poured yesterday. A small crack in the pavement, sort of like a hairline fracture, was the best I could come up with. I proceeded to shoot it from every conceivable angle.

Ronnie Berringer showed up a little before 2:00. I spotted him about half a block away. The first thing I noticed about him was that he was alone, which was good in that it would make it easier for me to talk to him, and bad in that a person choosing to have lunch alone probably had something on his mind.

The next thing I noticed about him was his coat. It was a dark blue overcoat. Not a gray parka. One in the plus column.

As he got closer, however, he started scoring in the minus column. He was walking slowly, mechanically, as if not really paying any attention to where he was going, or anything much else, for that matter. I'm admittedly not the best judge of people's states of mind, but I would have classed his as oblivious.

I decided to test the theory. I kept changing the angle on my picture taking so as to give him a good view of my face, just to see if he would recognize me.

He didn't. In fact, he didn't even see me. When I maneuvered in front of him he bumped right into me. Even then, he didn't really see me. He just murmured, "Excuse me," and would have kept on going if I hadn't called out, "Ronnie," and grabbed him by the arm.

Ronnie Berringer was about twenty-eight, and he still

had a boyish look. I remember my wife telling me a story Pamela told her about how when Ronnie first began working for the agency, he tried growing a mustache to make himself look older, then decided it was silly and shaved it off. I always thought it was a good story, because it summed up my impression of Ronnie Berringer: young and indecisive. In spite of that, he was a successful insurance agency executive, and probably earned four or five times what I did. Nonetheless, to me he always looked like a little boy.

Now he looked like a little boy lost.

His eyes focused on me, and I could see his mind going. "Who is this? Where do I know him from?" And then belated recognition: "Stanley."

"Yeah, hi," I said.

We grinned at each other stupidly for a couple of moments. When I realized he wasn't going to start the conversation, I did.

"What are you doing here?" I asked.

"I work here," he said.

"Here?"

"Yes." He pointed to the building.

"Is that right? I knew you worked somewhere around here, but I didn't know this was it. No kidding, you work right here?"

"Yes," he said. Then I guess it dawned on him since he had a reason for being here, that this was the question *he* should be asking *me*. "What are you doing here?"

I grinned some more. "I'm working here too."

"Oh?"

"Yeah. Right here. Not inside. Right here. See, a guy fell down here and broke his leg, and I'm taking pictures of the crack in the sidewalk he tripped on."

Ronnie looked. "What crack?"

For my money, it was the first genuine, normal response he'd made. His first real grip on reality. And I had to shatter it.

"Yeah." I pointed to the hairline fracture. "Right there."

He looked, then looked up at me incredulously. "Someone tripped on that?"

"Absolutely," I told him. "It may not look like much now, but when I get the right camera angle on it, it's gonna look like the Grand Canyon."

He blinked a couple of times, as if not sure whether to laugh or agree. Then, inspired, he looked at his watch and said, "Hey, I gotta go. Good seeing you."

"Yeah. You too."

He nodded, waved, and hurried through the door.

I stuck my camera in my pocket and headed for the subway. It hadn't been much of a meeting. I hadn't mentioned Pamela to see how he reacted. I hadn't even tried any subtle variations of the "where-were-you-between-the-hours-of-etc.-etc." gambit. But it was still enough to tell me all I needed to know about Ronnie Berringer.

He was scared shitless.

26

"YOU GOTTA GIVE UP Jane."

"What?"

I was sitting in the restaurant with Pamela Berringer again. I knew one thing for sure. This time I wasn't talking any moral philosophy and this time I wasn't taking any shit.

"I need to talk to Jane. You gotta tell me who she is."

"No."

"Don't tell me no, babe. I'm in the driver's seat now, and I'm crackin' the whip. I've got cops breathing down my neck every minute of the day. If I hadn't managed to ditch 'em just now, I couldn't even be talking to you. But I did, and I am, and while I'm on the loose I gotta make some moves, cause it may be the last chance I'll get. So you gotta give me Jane."

"No."

"If they get me, they get the tape. Don't you understand?"

"I know."

"How'd Ronnie seem last night? Pretty cool? Pretty loose? Nothing bothering him?"

She looked at me. Bit her lip.

"I don't know if you can take this much longer," I said. "But I'm telling you I can't. You're starting to crack up, so how do you think I feel? I need this settled, and I need it settled fast. Give me Jane."

"No."

"O.K. Then you tell me. Who took over? Who's running Darryl Jackson's girls."

"I don't know."

"Why not?"

"Because I don't *want* to know," she said fiercely. "Damn it. Don't you understand? I got out."

"And he never called you? Whoever took over?"

"No. He doesn't know about me. No one knows about me. And that's the way I want to keep it."

"No one's called you at all?"

She hesitated a second. "Yes. Jane called."

"And?"

"I told her to leave me alone. I told her I was out and I wanted to stay out. I read her the riot act. I told her not to tell anyone who I was. I told her if I got a phone call, it would be her neck. And I told her not to call me again."

"And more particularly, you told her not to let the guy know who you are. The guy who took over."

"Of course."

"And did she mention his name?"

"No."

"Then I gotta talk to Jane."

"No," she said. But weaker this time.

I tried to press my advantage. "There's no reason for you to protect Jane. She's the one who got you into this in the first place. She set you up, for Christ's sake, and—"

It was a mistake.

"No!" she said, strong again. "No, she didn't. It wasn't that way at all. She *did* fly to Indiana. And her mother *was* dying. She *did* die. All Jane did was tell Darryl Jackson she got someone to cover for her, so he'd let her go. And he took it from there. She had no idea what he was going to do. She was sorry as hell that it happened."

She stopped, sniffed, looked at me. "It's all true about Jane. Her mother. The kid. Everything. I can't give you Jane."

I looked at her for a long time. I sighed. "O.K.," I said. "If that's the way you want it. But if I don't come up with something soon, the cops are gonna haul me in and sweat it out of me. I have to tell you, though, I don't hold up well under interrogations. I might hold out a day, maybe two, but believe me, sooner or later they're gonna break me. And this much I do know: once you start talking, it's easy. You tell them everything. And once I start talking the shit is gonna hit the fan. You, Jane, the tape, everything.

"You're strong, you can take it. But it'll probably kill Ronnie. And I just hope it doesn't filter down to the school. I mean, Joshua's a bit young for stuff like that, but it's amazing what kids pick up, and—"

"Stop it!" she screamed. "Stop it! Goddamn you!"

Heads turned. I don't think there was a head that didn't turn. A waiter poised himself, in case action should be required.

"All right," I said. "Easy. Take it easy."

She had come half out of her chair. I got her seated back down. She grabbed the napkin, dabbed at her face.

"I'm sorry," I said gently. "I know that was very cruel. But it gives you an idea of how desperate I am."

She said nothing. Looked down at the table. I was trying to read her expression, but I couldn't quite catch it until I remembered the first thing I'd thought about her: her school girl look. She was pouting.

I leaned in to her. "Now listen," I said. "Jane will never know how I got on to her. She'll never know I got it from you. I promise you. Your name won't be mentioned. I'll keep you out of it. And I swear to god, I'll keep her out of it, too. I'm not going to hurt her, I promise you.

"But listen to me. There is more at stake here than some loyalty you feel you owe to some girl you knew vaguely from college, just because she's happened to have a hard time. You owe something to your husband, and something to your son. And, believe it or not, you owe something to me."

Tears were running down her face. She sniffed twice. Looked up at me.

"O.K.?" I said.

She sniffed again. "O.K."

"Good. Now tell me. How can I get in touch with Jane?"

I have to hand it to Pamela Berringer. She had a lot of spirit. Because she smiled slightly. It was a thin smile, but it was still a smile.

"Got a hundred bucks?"

27

It was moderately decent for an East Side hotel. Not real class, but not bad, either. The lobby was small, but clean. There appeared to be no dining room or bar. It was the type of hotel that catered to permanent residents. Any out-of-towner asking for a room for the night would have been laughed out of the place.

I walked up to the desk. The desk clerk put down his newspaper and looked at me.

"Can I help you?" he said.

"Room 357," I said.

"Your name, sir?"

"Jones."

He picked up the phone and rang the room.

"A Mr. Jones is here to see you."

He listened a moment, and hung up.

"You may go right up, sir," he said.

The clerk was quite deferential, and I didn't think it was all because of my suit. With a set-up like Darryl Jackson's, it was a cinch the hotel staff was getting greased with some heavy bucks.

I took the elevator up to the third floor, went down the hall, and knocked on the door of 357.

The door was opened by a young blond. She was Pamela's age, but not in Pamela's class.

I recognized her as one of the girls on the tapes. It was kind of weird. Sort of like having a centerfold come to life.

The thing was, the biographical data of the girls in the centerfolds always said something like, "cheerleader, likes Van Halen, wants to be in motion pictures." It never said, "single mother, child has Down's Syndrome."

I felt bad about what I was going to do to her, but I really had no choice.

"Mr. Jones?" she said.

"Yes. Jane?"

"Yes. Do come in."

I followed her into the room. It was your basic, simply furnished hotel room. It was clean and presentable, but obviously no one lived there.

The room was dominated by a king-size bed. Behind the head of the bed, screwed into the wall, was a huge mirror. Next to the bed was the door leading into the bathroom.

I stood there, looking at the bed. Jane came up to me.

"You said Darryl Jackson gave you my number?" she asked.

"Yes. A couple of weeks ago. I was gonna call, but something came up."

"I see," she said. "Look, I'd like to get the mercenary part over with so we can be friends."

"Suits me," I said.

I reached in my pocket and got out the five folded

twenties I'd got out of a cash machine on Broadway. The nice thing about using the cash machine was I didn't have to write it up in the check book as, "$100— hooker."

I passed the bills over to her. She took them and stuck them in her purse.

I pulled open my coat and flashed my I.D. at her, very briefly so she wouldn't notice that it was just an I.D. and there wasn't a badge.

"Ah shit," she said. "Not again."

She didn't argue or protest. She just slumped down on the bed in weary resignation.

I looked at her, and I realized her whole life had probably been like that. Just passively doing what she was told. No life. No spunk. I could understand Pamela Berringer not knowing her very well at college. She wasn't the type of girl other girls would want to know well. Nor was she pretty enough to have interested many of the college boys. But still she had been attractive enough to have made it as a high-priced call girl. It was probably her only accomplishment.

"You get knocked down often?" I said.

"No," she said. "And never in here."

"Well, there's a first time for everything," I said.

She shrugged philosophically. "Yeah, I guess so. All right. Where do we go?"

"We go to the bathroom."

She looked at me. "Huh?"

"Come on," I told her. "You're gonna like this."

She gave me a funny look, but she came.

On the wall of the bathroom, right behind where the head of the bed would be, was a large rectangular box jutting out from the wall. It was plastered over and painted up to look like the rest of the bathroom, but there was no structural reason for it that I could see.

"You know what this is?" I asked her.

"No," she said. "I guess its some heating pipes, or something."

"Could be," I said. "Come on."

I lead her back out of the bathroom.

"Come here," I said, and led her over to the bed.

"Oh, like that, is it?" she said.

"No. Not like that."

The mirror was fastened to the wall with twelve screws. I reached in my pocket, pulled out a screwdriver, and started taking them out.

Jane stared at me. "What the hell are you doing?" she said.

"I'm trying hard to resist any obvious puns," I told her. "Give me a hand, will ya? When I get these out, hold on to the other side of the mirror."

They came out easy. In a matter of minutes I was on the last one.

"O.K.," I said. "Now hang on, and set it down easy."

We lifted the mirror up and laid it down flat on the bed.

Behind the mirror was a hole in the wall. Behind the hole was the box I had seen fashioned in the bathroom. Inside the box was mounted a video camera.

I pointed to it. "Smile," I said to Jane. "You're on Candid Camera."

She goggled at me. "Huh?"

I groaned. "Oh Christ," I said. "Don't spoil my day by being too young to have heard of Allen Funt."

Jane was staring at the hole in the wall. "Hey, what is all this?"

"You don't know? Well, for your information, this is part of Darryl Jackson's little blackmail setup. You've been starring in his pictures, by the way. If you didn't know it, that makes you an unwitting accomplice. If you did know it, I guess that makes you a witting accomplice. At any rate, you're in bad. The question is, do you want to get out?"

She looked at me. "Huh?"

"Here's the thing," I told her. "The stakes are a little bigger here than you thought they were. Darryl Jackson was a slime and a blackmailer. Now he's dead. Someone else has taken over his prostitution racket. Frankly, I don't give a damn about that. What I want to know is whether he's taken over the blackmail end of it too."

She was looking at me, wide-eyed, desperate.

"I tell you, mister, I didn't know anything about this. I swear, mister."

"All right," I said. "You probably didn't. The thing is, now you do. And the question is, do you want to take the rap for it, or do you want to get out?"

She looked at me. "What are you saying?"

"I want the blackmail stopped," I said. "Now if the guy who took over for Darryl Jackson doesn't know about this setup, I got no problem and you got no problem. If he does, and he's using it, I'm gonna close him down. Now, *you* know about it. First, as a show of good faith, you're not going to tell him about it. Right? Second, you're going to tell me about him, so I can find out what he knows."

"But I don't *know* anything about him."

"You know his name, don't you?"

"Yeah."

"Well, what is it?"

"X."

"X?"

"Yeah. X."

"As in Malcolm X?"

"As in X."

"What's his real name?"

"I don't know. He likes to be called X."

"What's he like?"

"I don't know him very well."

"But you met him, right?"

"Yeah."

"So what's he look like?"

"Tough. Kinda scary looking."

"Black?"

She looked at me as if I were an idiot. "Yeah."

"How do you get in touch with him?"

"I don't. He gets in touch with me."

"You don't know where to reach him?"

"No."

"Can't you give me any more than that?"

"I tell you, I don't know very much about him."

"Well, who would?"

"Linda."

"Linda?"

"Yeah. Linda. She's his pet."

"How do you know that?"

"'Cause she went over to him *before* Darryl Jackson got killed."

"Oh yeah? How long before?"

"I don't know. Maybe a month."

"So tell me about Linda."

"Whaddya want to know?"

"Anything at all. What's her last name?"

"I don't know."

"How about a phone number?"

"I don't know that either."

"So how can I get in touch with Linda?"

"That shouldn't be hard. She'll be working here tonight."

"Tonight?"

"Yeah. Eight till midnight. That's her shift."

"I see," I said. I thought about that some.

Jane was looking at me closely. "Does that square things?"

"It's a start," I said. "What else can you tell me about Linda?"

Jane was eager to cooperate now that she saw a prospect of getting off.

"I don't know that much about her," she said. "But I can tell you this. She's tough. She won't sweat a hooking charge. I don't want shit like this on my record, but it don't bother her none. No skin off her nose. You tell her you're gonna haul her downtown, she'll just laugh in your face."

"So what *would* she sweat?" I asked. "How can I get to her?"

Jane shook her head. "I don't know. I told you I don't know her very well."

"You know her well enough to know that she's tough. You must know something else about her. Anything. Anything at all."

Jane thought a bit. "There is one thing," she said. "I don't know if it helps you any."

"Yeah? What is it?"

Jane shrugged. "She's a cokehead."

28

Rosa was standing on the corner of 48th and Broadway. I hadn't expected to find her there. It was early in the evening by her standards. I just swung by on the way down to her apartment on Avenue B, just on the off-chance, and there she was, large as life.

Rosa had helped me out during the Albrect affair. She hadn't wanted to, but I hadn't given her any choice.

In a way I'd done her a service, since the guys I'd "persuaded" her to help me nail had killed her boyfriend.

And in a way I hadn't, since those same guys happened to be the dealers who supplied her connection.

You see, Rosa was a cokehead.

It was 8:00 in the evening. After leaving Jane, I'd gone out, grabbed myself a quick burger, and sat there thinking about what to do next. I didn't want to go by my home or my office, where Sandy and the Professor might be hanging out waiting to pick me up again. I had to just stay out and keep on the move.

The one thing I had done was pick up my car. I was a little nervous about doing it. It occurred to me MacAullif might have traced my registration and got the license plate number, and had men staked out there to pick me up too. But I realized this was just paranoia. My car was parked a good three blocks away from my apartment house, and buried under a mound of snow. The license plate wasn't even visible. Even the sharpest detective on the force couldn't have found it.

Still, it made me nervous to do it. I kept glancing around me, looking for shadows the whole time it took me to dig the thing out. I needn't have bothered. The only person I saw was a black man with a shovel, who offered to dig me out for five bucks. I passed on the offer.

It took me forty-five minutes to do it myself. I had the motor running most of the time, so the trusty Toyota was all fired up and ready to go by the time I was through.

I pulled out and headed downtown. On the way, I swung by Broadway and 48th, just on the off-chance, and there she was.

I swung the car into the curb and got out.

I didn't know Rosa's last name. I knew her breasts though, and they were terrific. Now, of course, her figure was bundled up under the winter coat she wore over her working gear.

I walked up to her and said, "Hi."

She turned around with a welcoming smile. "Hi," she said.

Then she recognized me, and her face froze. "You."

It had only been a few months since I'd seen her last, but she looked older somehow. I guess hooking and drugs will do that to you. Still, she looked pretty good.

"Yeah," I said. "How you doing?"

I hadn't been quite sure of my reception, and it seemed she wasn't sure of it either. She was wary of me, and frankly I couldn't blame her.

"All right," she said. "Getting by."

"You mad at me?" I asked her.

"I don't know. Not really. Maybe a little," she said.

"I don't see why," I told her. "I did what I promised you. I left your connection in place."

"Yeah, but you cut off his source."

"I told you I would."

"Yeah," she said. "He was out for two weeks. I had to score on the street. Spent a lot of money on milk sugar and boraxo, you know what I mean?"

"That was a while ago. I'm sure he's back in business by now."

"Yeah." she said.

"His source killed your boyfriend, just in case you've forgotten. You really think he shouldn't have gone down?"

"I don't know what I think. I just do what I can and try to get by."

"Same as me," I told her.

"So, whaddya here for? Whaddya want?"

"I just wanted to talk to you a little."

"Oh yeah? What about?"

"About how you're doing. And what you're doing."

"Whaddya mean?"

"Like tonight, I mean."

She stared at me. "You don't know what I'm doing?"

"Yeah. I know what you're doing. I mean, you doing it for the same reason? You getting up money to score?"

"What do you think?"

"So how are you doing? How much you got so far?"

She shrugged. "A hundred bucks."

I looked at her. "Hey," I said. "We've been through this before, you know."

"All right," she said. "A hundred and fifty."

"And you need two hundred to score?"

"Yeah."

I'd taken the money back from Jane. I reached in my pocket and pulled out two twenties. I fished in my other pocket and pulled out a ten.

"Looks like you got lucky again."

She didn't take the money. She just looked at it. Then at me.

"What are you doing?" she said. "You mean you want to—"

"No," I said. "I'm not paying for your services. The money's for you."

She looked at me suspiciously. "Why?" she said. "What is it you want this time?"

I smiled at her. "You wouldn't believe me if I told you."

"Try me. Whaddya want?"

"I want a half a gram."

29

I MUST SAY, the clerk at the desk raised an eyebrow when I walked in.

"Room 357," I told him.

"Yes, sir," he said. "Your name again, sir?"

"Jones."

"Ah, yes. Of course."

He picked up the phone, called upstairs, and announced me.

"You may go right up, sir," he said.

It's hard to describe the look he gave me as I walked to the elevator. I've never known what it was like to have a reputation for a voracious sexual appetite before. Here comes the stud.

I took the elevator up to the third floor.

I had a half a gram of coke in my pocket, courtesy of Rosa, of course. I'd driven her over to her connection's townhouse on East 64th Street, just as I'd done months before in the Albrect case. I'd waited on the corner while she went in. Five minutes later she'd come back and given me a small plastic bag, just like the kind my father-in-law sells. In it was a small, carefully folded piece of paper with the half a gram.

197

After that, I'd given her a ride home to her apartment on Avenue B. Bumping into me hadn't been that bad for her. She was home early after a short working day, though a half a gram lighter than usual.

After that, I'd called Linda, made the appointment, and hustled back uptown. So, déjà vu. Here I was, once again, calling on a call girl.

Linda was a redhead. She was also a video star. I recognized her at once from the tapes. I didn't ask for her autograph, though. I just exchanged the usual pleasantries, and walked into the room.

I wouldn't want you to get the impression the only thing I know how to do is pull phony busts on hookers. But the thing is, when something works for you, you use it.

I didn't waste time with any preliminaries. As soon as we were into the room I whipped out the I.D., and said, "O.K., this is a bust. We're going downtown."

She stared at me, incredulously. "You out of your fucking mind?" she said. "What the fuck are you doing?"

"I told you. This is a bust. We're going downtown."

She still couldn't believe it. "What, are you nuts? What, are you green? Jesus Christ. That's no way to make a bust. No money's exchanged hands here. I haven't even *asked* you for money. You got no case against me."

"Doesn't matter," I told her. "I'll just say that you did. Nobody's gonna take your word for it."

She looked at me. "Are you shitting me?"

"Not at all. Come on. It's a bust, and we're going downtown."

"You're crazy, man. You're out of your mind."

"Not so's you'd know it," I said. I grabbed up her purse from the bed. "Here, let's see who you are."

She dove for it.

"You got no right to touch that."

"Uh uh uh." I said, turning my back to her and jerking away. "You wanna add resisting arrest and assaulting an officer to the charges? You just better keep cool."

I swung my back to her, so she couldn't get at it, and snapped open the purse. I reached my hand in it, and— sleight of hand—pulled out the bag with the half a gram.

"Well, well, well," I said. "Lookie what we got here."

Her eyes widened so much I thought they'd fall out of their sockets. "Well, of all the—" she said. "That's not mine. You planted it there."

I looked at her. "Hey, that's an idea. You could be right."

She looked at me as if I'd just told her the earth was flat.

"Huh?"

"You could be right," I said. "This coke could be yours, or it could be mine. I'm not sure. Let's think about it. Now, if it's yours, you're busted and we're going downtown. But if it's mine, you got nothing to worry about. And neither do I. If it's mine, it's mine, and I can do anything I want with it. In fact, I might even give it to you."

She was staring at me openmouthed now. "What?"

"Now, you're very lucky, 'cause it just happens that I need something. And you've got it. I want to know about X, and it just so happens that you know all about him, and you could tell me. And it ain't gonna hurt you none, 'cause he'll never know I got it from you.

"So that's the situation. Either this coke is yours, in which case we take a ride downtown and you get busted for drugs. Or, this coke is mine, in which case you talk to me a little bit, and then you take this coke home with you and you thank your lucky stars that you happened to meet me, and that when you did you happened to have something to trade."

"Are you serious?"

"Always. What we have here is the carrot and the stick." I held up the bag of coke. "This is the carrot. A half a gram of pure rock, guaranteed to be purer than anything you could ever lay your hands on. It is also the stick, cause if you don't take it, it's gonna take you, if you know what I mean."

She looked at me. "Whaddya wanna know?"

"X. I wanna know about X."

"What about him?"

"You were one of Darryl Jackson's girls. Now you're working for X. The thing is, you went over to X *before* Darryl Jackson got killed. That means you and X are pretty close."

"Yeah. So."

"So you must know a lot of things. And you know things that I want to know."

"Yeah. Like what?"

"First of all, what's his name."

She looked at me. "Jesus, you don't even know that? His name is Herbert Hoover Greene. He hates it. That's why he likes to be called X."

"Give me his home address and his phone number."

She did. I wrote it in my notebook.

"All right," she said. "What else you wanna know?"

"The thing I wanna know in particular is the connection. Between X and Darryl Jackson. Cause now Darryl Jackson is dead, and X is running all of Darryl Jackson's girls. So you tell me. What's the connection between X and Darryl Jackson, and how was he able to take over all his girls just like that."

"Oh."

"What's the matter?"

"I knew this was gonna be bad. I just didn't know how bad."

"You and X are pretty close, right?"

She made a face. "Look, let's get something straight. I hear this all the time from the other girls, but it's too much hearing it from you. X is nothing to me. He was the lesser of two evils, you know what I mean. X is a big, dumb, mean brute. Frankly, I don't like him.

"But Darryl Jackson was a slime. A real slime. Every week or so he'd have one of us up to his place for his own pleasure. And you know what he was into? Pain. Humiliation and pain. What got him off was seeing how low you could go, how much you could endure and still try to please him. And if you couldn't, you know, if it got too much to endure, and you couldn't go on, he'd slap you senseless until you did."

Her shoulders heaved and she looked at the floor. I could see tears start to come in her eyes.

Jesus.

I wondered if Pamela Berringer had gone through all that. She must have, I realized. It was hard to think about.

She sniffed, looked at me. "So you see how it is. X is

a dumb fucking brute. And he's mean and he's tough. If someone popped him tomorrow, I wouldn't shed a tear. But compared to Darryl Jackson, he's a fucking saint, you know."

I nodded. I was beginning to feel like an asshole for the tack I'd taken with her. For not treating her like a person. But I'd really had no choice.

"I see," I said.

"So there you are. And now you wanna know about X. Fine. I can tell you about X. I got no loyalty to him. I got no loyalty to anybody but me. Maybe if X went down, I could go on my own. Maybe. I got clients' names and numbers, you know. I got my own apartment, I don't need this room. Maybe . . ."

She snapped out of it, and her eyes got hard again. She pointed her finger at me. "But the thing is, you didn't get it from me. Anything I tell you about him, you didn't get from me. You hear me?"

"That's understood."

"O.K. Now, you want to know what the relationship was between X and Darryl Jackson, right? How he was able to take over all of Darryl Jackson's girls?"

"Yeah," I said. "Just tell me how he did it."

She smiled mirthlessly, shook her head, then looked up at me.

"He killed him, of course."

30

You KNOW, my self-esteem as a private detective has never been particularly high. But I try. I try hard. And in this case, I'd tried particularly hard. I'd protected my client, concealed evidence, played tag with the police, and painstakingly followed a trail of clues, trying to figure out who the murderer was. And through all of it, I'd tried to make sense of it, tried to put it together in my head, tried to do my Sherlock Holmes bit, and deduce what had happened.

And then I'm talking to some hooker, and she tells me who did it.

I blinked at her.

"What did you say?"

"He killed him, of course. What did you think? They've been rivals for years. When I went over to X, that was the last straw. That made it a blood feud. Darryl Jackson would have killed him if he got a chance. X just beat him to the punch."

"How do you know all this?"

"Are you kidding? He told me he did. He bragged to me. He's proud of it, you know?"

I looked at her. "You are gonna have to testify."

"Fuck I will," she said.

"Look here, you're talking to me—"

"Bullshit," she said. "I'm talking to you to get out of a drug rap. And because—well, if you get him, that's all right with me. But you said off the record and he would never know. Well, that's fine. But you put me on the stand and I'll deny this shit. Drugs or no drugs, I don't care how many phony counts you throw at me, I'm not talking. He'd kill me. He'd beat the rap. Somehow, some way, he'd beat the rap and he'd kill me. No way I'm doing that."

"If I put you on the stand—"

"If you put me on the stand, I'll not only deny it—I'll say I was with him at the time of the murder. I'll give him an alibi, and I'll make it stick. You don't get by in this business without learning how to tell lies. The jury will believe me and X will believe me. And you'll look like a fool."

"He can't just walk on this. I'm gonna nail him."

"Fine. You wanna nail him, you nail him, but leave me out of it."

"How am I gonna nail him without you?"

She looked at me. "Are you kidding? I told you he was dumb. You won't have any problem. He'll have made a hundred mistakes." She snorted. "Hell, he's so fucking dumb his fingerprints will probably be on the knife."

31

SHE FINGERED HIM for me too. I insisted on it. After all,
all she'd done for me was solve the case and tell me
who did it. I had to get some return for my half a gram.

Yeah, I gave it to her. If you think that makes me a
bad person, all I can say is you've probably never been
a murder suspect. I'm talking provocation here. That
and the ends justifying the means. The cops do it all the
time—supply dope to some junkie snitch to get on to
something big. Well, to be honest, I don't know that for
a fact. I'm just taking it from movies like "Prince of the
City." But I'd be willing to bet you it's true.

And the thing is, we all have our own morality and
our own code of ethics. And the way I see it, it would
have been worse to have promised it to her, and then
scammed her out of it, than to give it to her. In my
book, a deal's a deal, no matter what it is and who it's
with. Oh yeah, I would have no scruples at all about
scamming some rich, filthy dope pusher, but to scam
some poor, helpless junkie who was helping me out was
something else.

That's just how I see it. You don't have to see it that
way. But that's how I feel, and that's what I did.

At any rate, she rode uptown with me to a bar on Lenox Avenue in the 140's where she said X hung out.

She was right. He was there. She pointed him out to me through the window. She was being real careful not to be seen, and I couldn't blame her a bit. X was the type of guy for whom the phrase 'mean motherfucker' was invented. It wasn't that he was big—in that department, Darryl Jackson's next door neighbor had him beat hands down—it was just that he was solid. It was hard to tell where his head ended and his neck began. The man was a bull.

I put her in the car and drove her back downtown. She actually thanked me, which was quite unnecessary. She had kind of made my day.

I drove my car back up to the bar and parked outside. It was a moderately respectable bar, not posh, but not grunge either. I sized it up through the window. The first thing I noticed was that X was still there. If he hadn't been, I wouldn't have bothered to notice anything else. But having ascertained that fact, I took stock of the establishment. There was one thing I noticed immediately. Though the bar was fairly crowded, there wasn't a white man in the place.

I wouldn't want you to think I was getting any braver. I wasn't. I was scared to go into that bar. And I was scared of X. But I was scared of MacAullif too. And the thing is, when you got your balls in a vise, it ain't an act of bravery to try and get 'em out.

I took a deep breath and walked through the door.

For a second, I thought I was in a fucking western movie. Everyone stopped talking and looked at me. The bartender even stopped halfway through pouring a drink. I swear, if there'd been a honky-tonk piano, it would have stopped playing. The sheriff had just walked into the saloon.

The people in the bar had all jumped to the same logical conclusion. They thought I was a cop.

I was panicked, and I didn't know what to do. And I reacted the same way I had in the crack house. And that was to go with the rush of adrenaline, and cover the fear by coming off loud and aggressive.

I pulled open my coat, jerked the brown leather folder with my photo I.D. as a private detective about an inch out of my jacket pocket, and shoved it back in again, and said. "This is not a bust. I'm on stakeout up the street, nothing's happening, and I'm bored as hell and I want a beer. Anyone here points out I shouldn't be drinking on duty, I'm considering him drunk and disorderly and he's going downtown."

I thought that was pretty funny, but no one else seemed to. I found out how novice comics must feel working the late night audiences at the free gigs. Talk about a tough house. I didn't even get a smile.

I didn't try any more one-liners. I just walked over to the bar and slid in next to X. He gave me a look, then very deliberately swivelled around and gave me his back.

The bartender was democratic. He'd serve anybody with money, particularly when that person had the power to raid the joint.

X was drinking Schaefer, so that's what I ordered. The bartender brought me a bottle and a glass. I filled the glass, and put the bottle on the bar as close to X's as I could. There was about the same amount of beer left in each, which was good.

I chugged my glass of beer, hoping like hell Alice

would be sleeping when I came home smelling like a brewery, since I don't normally drink.

My glass had about an inch of beer in it. I held it up and looked at it appreciatively. With my other hand I surreptitiously reached under my coat and switched on my beeper.

Heads turned at the high-pitched "beep, beep, beep."

"Shit," I said.

I reached under my coat and switched the beeper off. I downed the beer in my glass, set it on the bar, then reached out and grabbed X's bottle by the tip of the neck. His back was still to me, and I don't think he noticed the difference. At any rate he didn't say anything. I got up and headed for the door.

The bartender tried to stop me. "Hey, you can't take that out of here," he said.

"Don't worry. I'll bust myself," I told him, and kept going. I'm not sure, but I think that time I might have gotten a chuckle.

I went out the door and hopped in my car. I gunned the motor, pulled out, and sped down Lenox Avenue. About ten blocks south I stopped, opened the car door, and poured the beer out in the street. I took one of my father-in-law's plastic bags out of the glove compartment, and put the bottle in it. I got out of the car and stashed the bag and the bottle in the trunk.

I got back in the car and drove home.

32

AFTER ALL THAT, the next day was pretty routine. At least it started out that way. I got up at 7:00, dug out my car, which took about a half an hour, and got on the road.

As expected, a whole mess of slip-and-falls had come in from the storm, which kept me pretty busy. Not only that, it was my day to turn in cases to Richard.

I drove down to the office, left my car in the municipal lot for an hour, I.D.'d my pictures and filled out my time sheets, and then rushed all the stuff down to Richard's office.

Naturally, I was looking out for Sandy and the Professor, though I didn't expect to see 'em. MacAullif would realize their cover had been blown, and if he still wanted me followed, he'd assign other men to the job. I pulled a couple of figure 8's on my way to the office just to see if anyone was tagging along. No one was. That meant one of two things, both of which were good: either MacAullif had given up on me, or he had taken the Congressman as bait.

I parked at a meter on 14th Street and went up to the office.

Wendy and Cheryl still hadn't forgiven me. In fact, their mutual dislike seemed to have formed a bond between them. They were more like the Bobbsey Twins than ever. They glared at me in unison, and it was a relief to finally get into Richard's office.

Richard wasn't his old self either. He seemed preoccupied while he went over the fact sheets.

"Sherry Webber, trip-and-fall, defective stair, fine, I'll take it; Matilda Mae Smith, super in her building, workman's comp, it's a washout; Juan Martinez, slip-and-fall in McDonald's, love to nail 'em, get some pictures some time when they're mopping the floor; Felix Pagan, hit-and-run, no-fault, I'll take it . . ."

He was done in record time. He didn't ask me a single question. He hardly looked at the accident photos, and didn't even notice I hadn't taken the pictures of Sherry Webber's stairs. This was unprecedented. Even more out of character, he gave my paysheets only a cursory glance.

When he was done, he pushed the work aside, leaned back in his chair, and looked at me.

"So," he said. "How's the case?"

"The case?"

"Darryl Jackson? The missing paper?"

"Oh, that case. I don't know. It's got nothing to do with me."

"So you said. I understand a Sergeant MacAullif called here looking for you."

"That's right."

"What did he want?"

"He just wanted to ask a few more questions. Try to sweat the truth out of me."

"Did he?"

"No, cause there's nothing to sweat."

"Really?"

"Hey," I said. "I can't lie to you. You're my lawyer."

Richard nodded. "Just so you remember that."

I finally got out of there. It was going to break Richard's heart if the truth ever got out, but I couldn't help that. I couldn't have given him what he wanted anyway. 'Cause I know the way he figured it, it only really would have counted if he could have gotten me off and I was really guilty.

I got out of there as quickly as I could, and headed out to my first assignment.

Before I got in the car, I did something I should have done earlier, but I hadn't had the time to do it. I called Leroy to thank him for bailing me out.

"No problem. Any time," Leroy said. "Why don't you stop by in your travels?"

"I'm rather booked up today. And I wouldn't want to lead the police to your door."

"It's as bad as that?"

"Worse."

"You must tell me about it some time."

"Yes. Perhaps when we're sharing the same cell."

"Speak for yourself," Leroy said. "I have no intention of doing time."

I said I wished I shared his optimism. I hung up, got in my car, and headed out.

My first assignment was way out in Hollis, Queens, so I had time to do a little mindless driving and a little thinking. Of course, the big question was what to do next. I had that bottle, and what I should do is take it in to MacAullif and see if the fingerprints on it matched up with the ones on the knife. But I realized that if I did that, I'd shoot my wad. I'd be out in the open with MacAullif. If the prints matched up, I'd be a hero. But if they didn't match up, or if there were no prints on the bottle at all, I'd be dead. 'Cause I'd have to explain, and there was no way that I could. It was just too big a risk to take, particularly just on the word of a hooker. I had to be sure.

I got off the Grand Central Parkway at 188th Street, worked my way down past Hillside Avenue, and found the address on Farmers Boulevard.

What with all the ice and snow, I was surprised to find that the client was a young boy who had fallen off his skateboard. It turned out he had stood on it in the living room. Why that entitled him to any money was beyond me, but someone must have thought so or I wouldn't have been there. Mine not to reason why. I had the mom sign the retainer forms, snapped the picture of the broken arm, and got the hell out of there.

I got back in the car and headed for my next assignment on Linden Boulevard in Brooklyn.

And started thinking again.

Yeah, I couldn't go to MacAullif without more proof. And I couldn't take Linda's word for it. I had to be sure. And the thing that was eating away at me was the only way to be sure, to be really sure, was to meet him myself. To talk to him. To confront him. To run a bluff on him, the way some fucking TV detective would have done.

And that is just what I couldn't do. 'Cause the plain simple truth was, I didn't have the guts. To stand up to that guy. To talk to him. I mean, hell, I'd seen him. The man was a murderer. Not only did I not want to talk to him face to face—it was more than that. I didn't want him to know who I was. To remember my face. To have it in for me.

I was in a hell of a mood as I pulled off the Grand Central and took the Interboro down into Brooklyn.

Coward, I told myself. You big, dumb, fucking coward. This is your chance, your one chance to get out from under. Now, this afternoon, while the cops are out chasing the Congressman, and no one's watching you, this is your chance. And you're not going to take it, are you? You know what you ought to do? You ought to go find him in that fancy bar he hangs out in in the afternoon, the one Linda told you about. You ought to walk right up to him and tell him you know he's a slime and a murderer. Look him in the eye and say, "I know you popped Darryl Jackson."

As I envisioned myself doing this, I got so paranoid I started shaking all over. I had to pull the car over to the side and stop.

Jesus Christ. If just the *thought* of doing it does this to me, what would *doing* it be like?

Not that bad, I told myself. He couldn't touch you in a crowded bar. There's nothing he could do. You'd be perfectly safe.

Yeah, sure. Safe. I'd be safe.

But so what? What did it matter?

The question was academic, anyway.

'Cause I was a bloody fucking coward, and I wasn't going to do it.

33

It was a fairly posh place on Third Avenue near 59th Street. He was standing at the bar talking to a gentleman in a business suit when I came in. I didn't want to butt in, so I hung out near the door and watched.

The businessman was pudgy and bald, and wore horn-rimmed glasses. He seemed to be very interested in what X had to say. They conversed for several minutes. Then X patted him on the shoulder, held up his hand, turned and walked toward the back of the restaurant. He seemed to be heading to the men's room, but when he reached the alcove leading to it, he stopped and turned toward the wall. His hand reached out toward the wall, left my line of vision, and reentered it a second later holding a telephone receiver. He fumbled in his pocket, pulled out what must have been a coin, and reached it out toward the wall. His arm then made little jabbing movements. He waited a few moments, then began talking into the phone.

It was a short call. He hung up the phone and returned to the bar, where the businessman was waiting. He said something to the businessman, who pulled out a pocket notebook, and wrote something down. He and the businessman shook hands, and the businessman smiled and left.

I strolled over to the bar. X had turned back to it, and was stirring the straw in his drink. I moved in next to him.

"Hi," I said.

His expression was pleasant enough when he turned to look at me. After all, I was probably a potential customer. But when he saw my face, his eyes narrowed slightly, and his brow furrowed.

I smiled at him. "You remember me, don't you?" I said. "You're just not sure from where. Let me help you out. I was in that bar in Harlem the other night, when you were having a drink. And now I'm in this bar and you're having a drink. Quite a coincidence, don't you think?"

He was looking at me deadpan, giving nothing away.

"Would you like to know why?" I asked.

His face might have been carved from stone. There was not even a flicker of response. I didn't let it bother me. I raised my hand, and motioned him toward me with my finger.

"Come here. I'll tell you."

He leaned in slightly. I leaned in too. I lowered my voice, but kept smiling, and said, conversationally, "I know you killed Darryl Jackson."

I think he blinked. If so, it was his only reaction. He just kept staring at me.

"I can prove it, too," I told him. "You see, I'm a private detective, and I'm investigating the murder. That's why I was there the other night. Checking you out. Sizing you up. I didn't want to bring this up there, though. I didn't think it would have been wise."

I can't describe the look he was giving me. And the thing about it was he was doing it without moving a muscle of his face. But what a look it was. I think if the bar had been any less crowded he would have killed me then and there.

I went on conversationally as if I didn't notice.

"Now the thing is," I said, "I could go to the cops, and they'd pick you up, and the case would be solved. My clients would be real happy. They'd think I'd done a hell of a job. But you know what I'd get out of it? Nothing. Zip. Time and expenses, just the same as if I'd failed. In fact, I'd make less, 'cause the case would be over and I'd be out of a job, whereas if the case dragged on for a while I'd still be on the clock.

"And the other thing is, if I go to the cops, they'll pick you up all right, but the charge might not stick. I got the proof, but you know what the legal system's like nowadays. There's still a good chance that you'd walk.

"But the thing is, it would cost you. 'Cause I'd have to tell 'em about your little prostitution racket. 'Cause that's the motive you see. You killed him to muscle in on his call girls. And you have. And it's a very profitable business. You're pulling in a small fortune from it, not to mention the shakedown bit on the side.

"So it occurred to me, here's a man with a multi-million dollar business going for him. And why should I blow it for him, just because it happens to be my job?

"Now, I know you don't want a partner, and I know you don't want to be bled dry, so I'll put it right on the line. What I want is $50,000. And it doesn't have to be all at once. It could be five- or ten-grand installments, spread out over however much time you say. And that will be it. The minute the last payment's made, I'm gone. I'm telling you this, because I know the first thing a guy like you worries about is it's gonna go on forever. So I just want you to know what the boundary is, and assure you that's as far as this is gonna go."

He still hadn't moved a muscle.

"So," I said. "Whaddya say?"

He stared at me a few moments more. "I don't know what you're talking about," he said, and turned back to the bar.

"Of course you don't," I told him. "I'm sure a guy like you kills so many people you couldn't be expected to remember killing one particular pimp. But trust me. You did. Just think about it, and I'm sure it will come back to you. In fact, I'm so sure it will, I'll call you at home later this afternoon to see if it did."

He picked up his drink. "I have an unlisted number."

"I know you do," I told him. "924-6352. Well, nice talking to you."

I got up to go.

"Just one thing," I added. "If for any reason you should try to follow me out of this place, I'm afraid I would have to yell cop."

He didn't even look at me. He took a sip of his drink.

I turned and walked to the door. Much as I hated to give him the satisfaction of seeing me do it, I couldn't help stopping and turning to look.

He wasn't following me. A businessman in a suit who had been waiting patiently all the while I'd been talking, had already taken my place. X was conversing with him freely and easily, as if nothing had happened. Just business as usual.

34

I FELT GOOD. Terrified, but good. Christ, I'd done it. I hadn't been half bad. I'd even sounded pretty tough.

I used to be an actor before I was a writer, before I was a private detective. And on opening night, there was always that terror that gripped you before the curtain went up, that moment of doubt when you thought, I won't know my lines, I won't know my part, I'm gonna freeze out there. And then when the curtain *did* go up, and you walked out on stage, you'd be calm, cool, relaxed, and everything would be all right.

It had been that way with X. I'd been cool as ice in that bar. Not a nerve in my body. I'd played the part, and played it well.

Now that the curtain had come down, however, I was back to my good old paranoid self, and I kept looking over my shoulder as I hurried over to Second Avenue where I'd left my car at a meter.

As I walked, I switched my beeper back on again. The beeper has a silent switch for when you're in some place where you don't want it going off, but you don't want to miss the call. You push the button halfway off.

Then, when you get outside, you push it back on again. If you've been beeped in the meantime it goes off, and if you haven't it doesn't.

It began beeping now. There was a pay phone on the corner, so I stopped and called the office. I must confess, the whole time I was still keeping a sharp lookout down the street.

Wendy/Cheryl had a new case for me in Brooklyn. I'd gotten it because presumably I was in Brooklyn, signing up my second case. Actually, I'd signed it two hours ago, as I was running way ahead of schedule. Now, having to go all the way back to Brooklyn, I'd be running behind. No matter though. If worse came to worse, I could call and stall the client. I said I'd take it.

I hung up, hopped in the car, got on the FDR Drive, and headed for the Manhattan Bridge.

I went over the bridge, took Flatbush Avenue into the Eastern Parkway, drove to East New York, and signed up a client on Mother Gaston whose kid had gotten lead poisoning from eating the plaster off the walls.

I got beeped while I was there, called in, and got routed out to Brookdale Hospital to sign up a guy who'd been in a motorcycle accident. Got beeped again, and sent back to sign up a slip-and-fall in a building on Halsey Street in Bed-Stuy.

By the time I finished all that, it was 4:30, which meant X should have had time to get home from the bar, and it was time to give him a call.

There are not that many pay phones on the street in Bed-Stuy, but I got lucky. I came out of the client's building and spotted one right on the corner.

Sometimes the phone booths are decoys. They look good, but when you get close you find out the guts have been ripped out. This one seemed to be fine. The only drawback appeared to be an old black bum picking through the garbage can on the corner. I detoured around him and picked up the phone.

It was working. Miracle.

I pulled out my notebook, and double-checked the number Linda had given me. I dropped a quarter in the phone rather than use my calling card number. This was one phone number I didn't want showing up on Richard's bill.

I punched in the number. It rang.

A gruff voice answered. "Yeah?"

"It's me," I said. "Have you thought over my proposition?"

"Yeah."

"So what's it gonna be?"

"All right," he said. "Five payments, $10,000 each spread out over six months."

I had him!

"That's fine," I said.

"Just one thing."

"Yeah?"

"That's provided you bring the proof."

"Don't worry. I'll bring it," I said. Then I realized that wasn't very smart. "But you get half now, and half after the last payment. Agreed?"

"Yeah. Fine. Just bring it."

"O.K. Where do I come?"

He gave me an address in Bedford Stuyvesant not three blocks from where I was standing.

"Wait a minute," I said. "That's not your address."

"That's right. You don't *go* to my address. Got it?"

"Yeah, I got it. What time?"

"Tonight. 9:00."

"You'll have the ten grand?"

"Yeah. Just you have the proof."

I hung up the phone. Hot damn, I thought. Hot damn!

The black bum had fished a broken toy plane out of the garbage can and was eyeing it covetously. As I hung up the phone, he turned his eyes to me. He wanted money, and I didn't want to give him any.

I have to explain. In New York City you can't walk half a block without a bum asking you for money. And the way I figure it, if I gave to one, I'd have to give to all. Otherwise I'd be discriminating: yeah, I like this bum, no, I don't like that bum. I can't afford to give to all, so I don't give to any. I admit this is a very self-serving philosophy—that's the whole point. And you may think that's heartless, and maybe you're right. But maybe you don't live in New York City.

At any rate, I saw the touch coming, and I wanted to avoid it. I tried to turn away.

He was too quick for me, that old man. He got in front of me, and thrust out his grungy hand. And I knew before he even opened his mouth what he was going to say: "Spare some change?"

He looked truly pitiful, and I hated to turn him down. He took a step toward me, snuffled twice, thrust out the expectant hand, and said, "MacAullif wants to see you."

35

"I't's called 'rough shadow/smooth shadow'."

MacAullif leaned back in his chair and looked at me. I was trying to look anywhere else but at him. I felt foolish as hell.

"It's a fairly routine tactic," MacAullif went on. "I would expect most private detectives would be familiar with it. But then you're not like most private detectives, are you? No. You're a gifted amateur."

MacAullif took out a cigar, bit the end off it, and surveyed it with some distaste.

"Naturally, as you by now have figured out, what I told you, though essentially true, was also a trap. I wanted to see what you'd do. So I called you into my office, gave you the speech, and put a tail on you. And what did you do? Nothing. We followed you all over Queens and Long Island, and all you did was carry out your business as usual and went home.

"That's when we decided to force the game. The rough shadow let you get a glimpse of him. You proceeded to ditch him in relatively routine fashion, and went about your business. That, of course, was where the smooth shadows took over. And sure enough, things began to happen. First you called on Congressman Blaine. Then you led us to a housewife named Pamela Berringer. What we wanted, of course, was for you to lead us to your client. And the first day we had it doped out wrong. We figured the Congressman for the client. After all, that was the natural way to figure it. He was the guy with the money and position, the guy who could afford to hire a private dick. He was also the type of guy who couldn't afford a scandal. Whereas Pamela Berringer was just your normal, everyday housewife. So we picked the Congressman for your client, and Pamela Berringer as just a witness.

"The next day straightened things out. You went to see the Congressman without bothering to ditch the rough shadow. So we knew right away the Congressman was a red herring, and someone that for some reason you wanted us to pick up on.

"You then ditched the rough shadow and called on Pamela Berringer, which confirmed the fact that *she* was the one you were trying to keep us away from, and therefore the client.

"En route to meeting Pamela Berringer, you contrived an impromptu meeting with a young man who, on investigation, turned out to be her husband, further confirming the fact that she was the client, and establishing the fact that her husband didn't know it.

"After that, we dropped the rough shadows and stuck with the smooth, giving you the impression that we had either taken the Congressman as bait, or had given up.

"We then proceed through a myriad of events. In between conducting your business for Rosenberg and Stone, you contacted a young woman who happens to have a record as a call girl. Then you contacted a street hooker, with whose assistance you managed to score a quantity of drugs which we presume to be cocaine. You then contacted another call girl, and accompanied her to a bar. After she left, you proceeded to go inside and hassle some black man, following which you appropriated a bottle of beer. The following day you approached the same black man in another more posh establishment, and engaged in a conversation which left the gentleman in question somewhat less than pleased. You then spent the rest of the day calmly carrying on the normal course of your business."

MacAullif pointed the cigar at me.

"Now," said MacAullif. "Let me emphasize right here that we, the police, have not done anything illegal. We haven't searched your home or your office, or tapped either of your phones. All we've done is conducted a perfectly legal surveillance, which was certainly justified under the circumstances.

"You, on the other hand, are guilty of possession of a controlled substance, conspiracy to purchase a controlled substance, sale of a controlled substance, transporting an opened alcoholic beverage from its place of sale, withholding evidence, obstructing justice, accessory after the fact to murder . . ." He broke off, "Must I go on?"

"I'd rather you didn't."

"Now, having said all that, I'm sure you can understand the position you're in. I don't think I have to advise you of your rights, but, of course, I do. You understand that you don't have to say anything that might incriminate you, and you also have the right to an attorney. Would you like to call one?"

I thought of Richard. Of what he'd make of all this. "No," I said.

"Fine," he said. "In that case, having been duly warned, do you have anything you'd like to say?"

I reached in my pocket and fished out my car keys.

"Here's the keys to my car," I said. "You know where it's parked. In the trunk you'll find a plastic bag with a beer bottle in it. If the fingerprints on that bottle should happen to match the ones on the knife, we'll talk."

36

I**T'S ALWAYS PAINFUL** to find out you're an asshole. Particularly when you thought you were being so smart. It happens to me a lot, though. But usually it happens over the course of some time. I'll look back to something I did a couple of years ago and think, boy was I an asshole then. Of course, this was a slightly tougher kind of realization to handle. This was, boy am I an asshole now.

I should have known it was too easy walking away from my shadows. Hell, I knew MacAullif was smart. But I'd played him for a sucker, and wound up playing myself for a sucker instead. I'd botched everything up from the word go, and, once again, I had fucked myself.

And the thing about it was, there was nothing I could do about it but sit, wait, and pray that the fingerprints matched up.

They did.

37

"It's not enough."

I stared at MacAullif. It's hard to take when your prayers are answered, and it still doesn't do you any good.

I'd told MacAullif everything. Except, of course, about the video tapes. That was something no one was ever going to know. But I'd told him about Linda and X. The fingerprints had matched, and I'd thought I was home free.

And now this.

"What do you mean, it's not enough?" I said.

MacAullif shrugged. "It's a good case, but not a convicting case. With the girl's testimony it would be, but we won't get that. You know it and I know it."

"But the prints on the knife."

MacAullif waved it away. "Yeah, yeah, the prints on the knife. The guy knew Darryl Jackson, he had dinner with him the week before, he helped him carve the roast. You know what some smart attorney will say. Plus this guy will have eight or ten hookers ready to swear that he was with them the whole time in question. Believe me, we'd be lucky to get a hung jury."

"But he did it."

"Sure he did it. You know he did it, and I know he did it. And that and fifty cents will get you a cup of coffee. At least it would last week, I don't know, everything's going up all the time."

"So what are you gonna do? You can't let it drop."

"No. I can't let it drop."

"So whaddya do?"

MacAullif shrugged. "We don't have enough evidence, we get more evidence."

"How?"

"We nail the son of a bitch."

"How?"

"We get him to confess."

I stared at him. "How the hell you gonna do that?"

"With a wire."

"What?"

"With a wire. We nail the fuck with a wire. We get someone to talk to him with a wire on. Get him to admit he did it. Get it on tape. Then we got him dead to rights."

"Sounds good to me," I said. "When are you gonna do it?"

"Tonight."

"Great," I said. "It's a big load off my mind. Who's gonna wear the wire?"

"You are."

38

OF COURSE, I had to wear the wire. I made the contact. I made the blackmail approach. It was a natural. I was perfect for the role. Except for one thing. It was gonna take a lot of guts.

MacAullif knew I didn't have 'em.

"We'll be right behind you," he said. "There's nothing to worry about. We'll be listening to every word. The moment it gets hairy, bam, we're there."

I had my shirt off. A detective was taping the microphone to my chest. He ran a thin wire down to my navel.

"Drop your pants," he said.

"This so you can add indecent exposure to your list of charges?" I asked MacAullif.

"Charges? What charges?" he said.

"Right," I said. "When you nail me for blackmail and extortion, I want you to know the same goes double for you."

"Blackmail? Extortion?"

"Well, coercion then."

"Ah, coercion." MacAullif smiled and shook his head. "Hardly the same thing. Don't give it a thought."

"What are the N.Y.P.D. regulations about running private citizens as decoys with wires?"

"I don't know the exact specifications. You want me to look it up?"

"I didn't know you could read."

"Yeah, well I got some pretty bright cops on my team. One of them went to high school."

The detective had run the wire under my balls, up the crack of my ass, and was now taping the case to my back.

"This guy enjoy his work as much as he seems to?" I asked MacAullif.

"Ah, he's a good man," MacAullif said. "I think he's only electrocuted one cop working a wire."

"That's reassuring to know," I told him.

I realized the jive patter was just to keep my spirits up. I also realized it wasn't working. I was scared shitless.

The guy finished taping the wire.

"O.K.," he said. "You can put on your shirt."

I did, and pulled up and buckled my pants.

"O.K.," he said. "Let's give it a test. Say something."

"Whaddya want me to say?"

He reached behind my back and pushed something. A second later I heard my voice say, "Whaddya want me to say?"

He clicked it again. "All set," he said.

The detective went out. MacAullif reached in his pocket and pulled out a small manilla envelope.

"What's that?" I said.

"You told the guy you had evidence," said MacAullif. "This is it."

"What is it?"

"It's a tape recording of him telling a hooker he popped Darryl Jackson."

I stared at him. "What?!"

"It's a mock-up, of course. We threw it together while they were fixing the wire."

He opened the envelope and slid out a micro-cassette. He took a miniature recorder out of his pocket, opened it, and popped the tape in.

"There was no way we could match up his voice," MacAullif said. "So we lead with the hooker. See?"

MacAullif pushed a button. There was a burst of static, then I heard a girl's voice say, "Gee, X, you're so smart. Tell me how you managed to take over all of Darryl Jackson's girls." Then a black male voice said, "Shit, nothing to it."

MacAullif snapped it off.

I looked at him. "That doesn't sound a bit like him."

MacAullif shrugged. "I didn't think it would."

"Who's the hooker?"

"Stenographer."

"It's worthless," I told him. "The minute the guy hears this, he's gonna know it's a plant."

"It doesn't matter," said MacAullif. "See, this tape is the signal. The minute you pop this on, we come in."

"What if he hasn't confessed by then?"

"He has to have confessed by then. That's the whole thing. See, the way we figure it, unless he popped Darryl Jackson, there's no reason in the world for him to go so far as to listen to the tape."

"Yeah, but—"

"And that's your job," MacAullif said. "It's up to you to make sure he does confess before you turn on that tape."

I didn't look convinced.

MacAullif grinned. "That shouldn't be hard for a gifted amateur like you."

39

IT WAS A FOUR-STORY BUILDING in the middle of the block with an alley running along one side. I cruised by it once, just as I would have done if it had been a potentially risky signup. And in my mind I played the game again: how bad is it going to be?

Not that bad, I told myself. And told myself. And told myself.

Yeah, not that bad. MacAullif and half-a-dozen cops would be right behind me. They'd park on the next block, and move in as soon as I got inside. And I was wearing the wire, so they'd know what was happening all the time. By the time I got into the apartment, they'd be in the building. At the first sign of trouble they'd move in.

So what could go wrong?

Well, they could burst into the room and find a dead private dick lying on the floor. Cut it out. Asshole. Just tell yourself it's a signup. It's a signup, just like any other assignment. You diddle the guy, hand him a bill of goods, and close the deal.

Yeah. That's the idea. Treat it as a signup. Shit,

maybe even snap his picture. Christ, what are you thinking that for? You're getting punchy. You can't afford to lose it now.

I circled the block and pulled up in front of the house. I got out of the car. It felt funny getting out of the car without my briefcase. How can I treat this as a signup without my briefcase? Imagine the briefcase, asshole. You were an actor—what would Stanislavski say? Fuck him. Who cares. It's memory of emotion, not memory of briefcase. Why are you thinking that now? Oh yeah. Signup. Briefcase. Right. Pretend you got a briefcase. Just don't get carried away and pantomime the damn thing.

I went up the front steps. The front door was unlocked. I pushed it open and went in.

I found myself in a dimly lit foyer facing a narrow staircase. No one was in sight. I took a breath and started up the stairs.

X had said apartment 3R. Here I go again. Did that mean third floor right or third floor rear? Pick a door, any door. Behind one door you'll find a psychotic murderer who'll want to kill you for attempting to blackmail him. Behind the other door you'll find a mystery guest, who may or may not be friendly. Or would you rather quit right now and keep the felony counts of suppressing evidence and accessory to murder?

I reached the third floor landing. No choice. The door to the right was also to the rear. I went over to it, raised my hand.

Whose apartment was this? Why had X wanted to meet me here? Did some friend of his live here? Or was this some apartment he maintained just so he'd have a place to use when he wanted to rub someone out? Nonsense. He wouldn't want dead bodies showing up in some apartment with his name on the lease. What lease? Maybe it's not his apartment. Maybe it's a vacant apartment. Maybe he just broke in here to use it. Then how did he know the address just like that? He must have used it before. For what?

Yeah. Maybe it's a friend's apartment. And maybe the friend's there. Maybe a lot of friends are there. So many that MacAullif and the boys won't make any difference. It'll be over before they get there. They'll nail X all right, but not in time to do me any good. "PRIVATE DETECTIVE MURDERED: The body of Stanley Hastings, a private investigator, was discovered late last night by homicide detectives, who—"

Stop it. Asshole. What was it MacAullif said? No one stands in the hallway for five or ten minutes. There's the door. The curtain's going up. It's showtime.

I knocked.

There was a moment's silence, and to me it seemed as if it were the answer to my most fervent prayers. He wasn't there.

Then footsteps.

And the door opened.

X stood in the doorway. He had changed out of his suit into a sweatshirt and blue jeans. His killing gear? His face had that stolid, impassive look that seemed to be his only expression.

"Come in," he said.

Never have I had a less appealing invitation.

X stepped back out of the way to let me pass. I didn't like that. I didn't want to put him between me and the door.

But there was no help for it. The play had begun and

the stage direction said, 'private detective crosses into room.' Or perhaps the director had given that stage direction in rehearsal, in which case I would have pencilled it into my script. In which case, the shorthand notation for "cross" would be "x," and I would have written "x into room." and in this case "x by X into room."

Oh god, I *am* losing it. I got through the bar scene, but this is too much. I'm cracking up. I'm going routines again. Shit. Hold together. Whatever you do, just don't start talking out loud to yourself.

I walked into the room. It was a sparsely and cheaply furnished living room. No props. Nothing in the room I could put my finger on and identify as a sign of human occupancy.

Not a home.

A stage set.

A killing ground.

Sound from offstage left: click of X turning the deadbolt, locking the door.

X x's into room.

Stop it! Schmuck! Stop your mind! This is real, and this is here, and this is now. Do it. Play the scene.

Scene. Shit! Your mind's in a loop. Get it out.

X: (*ominously*): "You bring the proof?"

ME: "I got it. You got the money?"

X: "Yeah. Let's see your proof."

ME: (*reaching in pocket and—*)

Shit! Last chance. Pull yourself together.

My head was spinning. I shook it to clear it. I reached in my pocket and pulled out the envelope. I opened it and slid out the micro-cassette.

"What's that?" X said.

This was it. My big speech. I looked him in the eye.

"It's a recording of you telling a hooker how you popped Darryl Jackson. The hooker was wearing a wire. Lucky for you, the hooker wasn't working for the cops, she was working for me. So instead of going up for the big one, all you gotta do is come across with fifty G's."

His eyes widened. "Son of a bitch."

His hand fished in his back pocket, came out a second later. I heard a click. I looked, and saw I was staring at an eight-inch ugly switchblade.

Which wasn't in the script.

I didn't have my confession yet, but I didn't care. At that moment, all I wanted to do was get out of that room alive. I had to signal MacAullif, and the best way was the direct way. Fuck the script. Time to improvise.

"Hey," I ad-libbed. "What the hell you doing with that knife?"

He started across the room for me.

"I'm gonna stick you, just like I stuck Darryl Jackson," he said.

I was so fucking scared that for a moment I didn't even realize I'd just got what I'd come for. Then it dawned on me. I had him.

But he also had me. Come on, MacAullif, you dumb fuck. He just said the magic word. That's your cue. Where the fuck are you?

Something hit the door hard. In a play, three cops would have burst into the room. But this wasn't a play, and X had one strong fucking door. It didn't give at all.

He turned at the sound, though, and that was the one break I needed. I lunged for the window. There was no time to open it. I flung out my arm, smashed the panes of glass with my hand. I brushed them aside and tried to fling myself up and over the sill. I caught a quick glimpse of what was outside. Three stories down and no fire escape. Well, fuck it, who cares? So I break my damn leg. I'll sign myself up and sue the owner of this fucking building, just let me out of this damn room.

I was half-on half-off the sill, squirming out the window. I teetered over the edge and started down.

A hand gripped my ankle, caught and held. I slammed into the side of the building from the force. I looked up. A huge black face glared down at me. He had my leg in his left hand. In his right hand he had the knife. And he was reaching down to plunge it into my back.

A nightstick crashed against the side of his head. His eyes widened, his grip loosened, and suddenly I was going down. What, no stunt man? That's movies, not plays, schmuck, and—

I hit the ground and rolled over in finest paratrooper fashion, which was rather lucky for me, having never been a paratrooper. The snow was deep, which probably helped a lot.

I looked up and saw MacAullif standing in the window. Scared as I was, shaken as I was, I could not resist the childish impulse to *be* one of those fucking TV heroes, those cocky pricks who toss off an adventure like this every day after breakfast, and always have some jive rejoinder waiting.

So I raised a finger, waggled it at him like one actor commenting on a fellow actor's performance, and called up to him, "Little slow on the entrance."

"We'll work on it," he called back. "You all right?"

"Fine." I told him.

I was too. I got to my feet. I'd have a few bruises, and I saw now that my wrist was cut from where I'd smashed through the window, but, basically, that was it.

Tough luck, Richard. There goes our million dollar lawsuit.

Tag line:

Some days you just can't get a break.

Curtain.

40

IT WAS 2:00 in the morning before the cops got everything sorted out and I finally got home. When I did,
there was no place to park. The snow had jammed up
everything. Some people had been lucky enough to
back into dug-out spots, but a lot of others hadn't. Out
of desperation, many drivers had beached themselves
by driving into the huge drifts the snowplows had left
along the sides of the street, and faced the task of
attempting to dig themselves out the next morning.
Cars were parked crisscross, diagonally, every which
way. Every available inch of space was taken.

Great, I thought. "Super-sleuth solves case, can't park
car." When I'd solved the Albrect case, I'd gotten a
parking spot just like that. Well, you can't win 'em all.

I circled the blocks, hoping for a miracle, and thinking about how things had turned out.

Well, another case wrapped up, and, once again,
without earning a fee. I may be getting a little better as
a private detective, but as a businessman, I'm the pits.
I'll have to sit down with a calculator some day and see
how much, what with gas, tolls, VCR rental, TV pur-

chase, taxi fares, and fifty-dollar cash bribes to hookers, solving this case had actually cost me. Not to mention, of course, the hours I had to take off from my real job.

I thought about Tommie's tuition, Con Ed, and the phone bill. It was not a happy thought. Well, tax time would be rolling around, and with the year I've had, I should be due for a refund. If we're not evicted by then, I'll pay the rent.

A car's headlights snapped on a half-block away. I instinctively gunned the motor, skidded, fishtailed, and nearly side-swiped a parked car. I must have been really tired. I mean it's not as if someone else was gonna ace me out of the spot. There wasn't another car for blocks.

The car I'd seen turned out to be one of those that had been bunged up into the drift. It took the driver 20 minutes to get it out, even with a shovel and with me getting out and pushing, which I sure as hell did. I was so pumped up by the time the car finally lurched out of the drift, that if anyone had come along and tried to park in that spot, MacAullif would have had another chance to nail me for murder. Fortunately, no one did. I pulled by the space, gunned the motor, cut the wheel, and slammed backward into the drift. The car teetered on the brink for a moment. Then the wheels grabbed, and I slid back and in.

I killed the motor and killed the lights. Then I slumped forward, exhausted, on the steering wheel.

Well, I'd done it. "Private detective conquers fear— extradites self from holy mess." Had I really conquered fear? Well, I hadn't peed in my pants when X pulled the knife—that was something. But I hadn't taken the knife away from him, given him a spanking, and handed him over to MacAullif, either. Instead, I'd jumped out a window, which, I guess, lay somewhere in between. Well, I suppose it's a start.

I got out of the car, went into my building, woke up the elevator man, and had him take me upstairs. I unlocked the door and let myself into the apartment. Alice had left the foyer light on for me.

I pulled off my boots, and took off my coat and my tie and jacket, or what was left of them after my brush with X. Add the cost of a suit and coat into my list of debits.

I tiptoed down the hall and looked in on Tommie. He was sleeping soundly in his Keith pajamas—dressed as one of the Space Explorers from Voltron.

I went into the bedroom. Alice had left the reading light on for me. She was sleeping, of course, but she was tossing and turning fitfully, and making grunts and groans. I realized for the first time how hard all of this had been on her. It's tough when you get so caught up in something, and then you realize you're not thinking about anybody else but yourself.

I leaned over and put my hand on her shoulder.

"It's all over," I whispered. "The cops got the guy who did it. I'm out of danger. Everything's all right."

I swear she was asleep. But when I said it, she rolled over and lay quiet.

41

THERE WERE A FEW LOOSE ENDS to tie up.

I stopped by MacAullif's office the following afternoon to make sure everything was squared away.

"Pamela Berringer is out of it," MacAullif assured me. "Her name has not been mentioned, and it won't be mentioned. Nor will she be hassled in any way. Consider the matter dropped."

I thanked him.

"No need to thank me. We just happen to have the matter tied up, and she doesn't happen to be involved. But, just between you and me, you know and I know she's a hooker, and she happens to be the Skirt. And in all probability, her husband is the Parka. Now all of that paints a nice little picture, but it doesn't happen to be one that concerns me."

"What about the Congressman?"

"What *about* him?"

"Well, what are you gonna do about him?"

"Nothing. He didn't kill him. He's not involved."

"He found the body. He didn't report it."

"So did the Skirt and the Parka," MacAullif pointed out.

"There's a difference."

"I fail to see it."

"The Skirt and the Parka have never been questioned by the police. The Congressman has. And he lied. The most you have on the Skirt and the Parka is failing to report a crime. But the Congressman lied to the police in an official investigation. That's obstructing justice. It's a huge difference."

MacAullif looked unhappy. "I suppose you could look at it that way."

"Well, how the hell *do* you look at it?"

MacAullif was a big man and a tough man, and somehow I couldn't picture him squirming. But he was.

"Listen," he said. "Sometimes there are things about my job I don't like."

I stared at him. "Are you telling me you've been ordered to lay off?"

"No," he said. "I'm not telling you that."

"But you have, haven't you?"

He said nothing.

"I don't believe it," I said. "After all that crap you fed me about being a sergeant all your life and not swallowing the department line, you're gonna let the Congressman walk. I guess that was all horseshit, right? All part of the trap? You never meant it at all."

He whirled on me. "Son of a bitch! You know I meant it. Just between you and me the Congressman's a slime. And I tell you, if I had anything on him, anything at all, orders or no orders, I'd nail his ass to the wall."

"But you do. You've got a witness."

"What witness?"

"Celia Brown."

"Yeah." He looked at me. Sighed. "Celia Brown is dead."

I stared at him. "What?"

"Yeah. She's dead."

"My god. How'd it happen?"

MacAullif twisted the cigar in his hands. I could feel the anger in him.

"Well," he said. "I told you she was a junkie. Well, you know how it is with a street hooker who does drugs. She turns tricks all day to get the money to score. Then her pimp comes along and beats her out of most of it. So she never has enough to score much dope at a time. Just enough to keep the monkey off her back, keep her going another day. So, as near as we can piece it together from talking to some of her street friends, this is what happened. Day before yesterday she finishes her day's work, her pimp rips her off, she gets ready to score. And what should happen, but a guy comes along and lays five hundred bucks on her. It's a windfall to her. She's never had that much money of her own at one time, not that her pimp didn't know about.

"So she guys skag. A lotta skag. Not just enough to get along. For once she's gonna have herself a good time.

"So next morning an O.D.'d junkie hooker shows up in the morgue. We didn't I.D. her till late last night. I just found out this morning."

I stared at him. "That's murder," I said.

"Sure it is," he said. "But it's one that's impossible to prove. Even if we could I.D. the Congressman as the guy who gave her the money—and we can't—there's no case. And without Celia Brown's testimony there's no case against him on the other thing. So that's that."

I sat there, feeling slightly lower than shit. I looked down at the floor. Then I looked up at him.

"I have to tell you something. I'm the one who told the Congressman the cops had a witness. I told him the first time I saw him. I was trying to get a rise out of him. Running a bluff. It was my fault. I'm an amateur and I made a mistake."

"Well," MacAullif said, "the pros ain't so good either. I told him the same thing."

I looked at him. "For real?"

"Yeah, for real. So take your penny-ante guilt and shove it, mister. It happened to you once. Just for your information, it happens to me all the fucking time."

MacAullif shook his head. "All right, look," he said. "I'll tell you something. Off the record. I've got orders to lay off. But I'll tell you something else. If I had anything, anything at all, I'd nail that fuck to the wall."

I was hopelessly torn. Talk about a moral dilemma. MacAullif didn't know about the tape. If I told him, he'd go after the Congressman. I was sure of it. But Pamela Berringer was on the tape, and I'd have to give her up too.

I couldn't do it. Even if MacAullif promised her immunity all the way, I couldn't do it. Some crazy, prehistoric, macho instinct in me that I didn't even know I had, and that Pamela Berringer certainly wouldn't even have appreciated, made me feel it was my duty to protect her, told me I couldn't even let MacAullif *see* that tape of her, whether he did anything with it or not.

So what the hell could I do?

"So that's it," I said. "The police look the other way and the Congressman walks."

"If you want to put it that way, yeah."

"It's not right," I said.

MacAullif snorted. "Tell me something new."

"All right," I said. "Legally, there's nothing we can do about the Congressman. But the son of a bitch shouldn't get off scott free. The son of a bitch ought to pay."

"No argument here. But it's not gonna happen."

"I know. The police look the other way and he walks."

"I wish you'd stop saying that."

"Suppose," I said, "it were the other way around."

He looked at me. "What do you mean?"

"Suppose the police looked the other way and he paid?"

He frowned. "What the hell are you talking about?"

"Well," I said. "Speaking hypothetically now, suppose, just suppose, there was a way to make him pay. Providing the police did nothing about it. Would that interest you?"

"That would interest me a lot," MacAullif said. "Hypothetically, of course."

"Of course."

"Yeah," he said. "Hypothetically speaking, I would like to know how that could be done."

I told him.

42

"I DID YOU A SERVICE, and I want to get paid."

Congressman Blaine regarded me as if I'd just crawled out from under a rock.

"Let me make something clear," he said. "The reason I let you in here today was to tell you I don't want to see you again. If you call on me again, you will not be admitted. If you make a nuisance about it, I will call the police."

"That's a very noble sentiment," I said. "And I understand it entirely. I have no intention of ever calling on you again."

"I'm glad to hear it."

"But I'm calling on you now. I did you a service, and I want to get paid."

"I don't know what you're talking about."

"You know what I'm talking about. The Darryl Jackson murder."

He looked at me. "It was on the radio. They arrested some punk for it. The Darryl Jackson case is solved."

"I know. I solved it."

"That's not the way I heard it."

"Yeah, well that's the way it happened."

"So what? I tell you, the Darryl Jackson case has nothing to do with me."

"I know that. That's why I told you I'd keep you out of it. That's the service I did you. I kept you out of it."

"You didn't keep me out of it, you son of a bitch. You sicked the cops right on me. I had to pull some pretty fancy strings to convince them I wasn't involved."

"Don't blame that on me," I said. "I didn't tell the cops a thing about you. I told you, they had a witness. That's how they got onto you. I kept you out of it. That's the service I did you, and that's why I expect to be paid."

"Well, the service was ineffective, and payment will not be made. I never requested any service and I never promised any payment, if you'll recall."

"That's a bad attitude to take," I told him. "The case may be solved, but there's other matters to be tied up. They can't get you for killing Darryl Jackson, mainly because you didn't, but you did search his apartment, and you lied to the police about it. That's breaking and entering, suppressing evidence, obstructing justice, and makes you an accessory after the fact to murder."

"You can't prove that."

"The police can. They have a witness."

"They don't have a witness. She—" He cut himself off, but it was enough. It was all I needed to hear to convince me that he'd done it. To make me not feel guilty about what I was about to do.

"Not talking to the cops was only a part of the service," I said. "If you'll just bear with me a minute."

I got up from my chair and reached in my coat pocket.

"I see you have a VCR here," I said, walking over to it.

I pulled the video tape out of my coat pocket.

"I have a tape here I think you ought to see."

I punched the VCR on and hit the eject button. A tape popped out.

"Front-loading. Classy," I said.

I shoved in my tape. Turned on the TV. Hit the play button.

There was the usual burst of snow, then the picture of Congressman Blaine and Pamela Berringer filled the screen.

I let it play for a few seconds, then hit the stop button, and pressed eject.

I took the tape out of the machine. I walked over and laid the tape on his desk.

He was staring at me expressionless, poker-faced, like a player waiting to hear the next bet.

"This is the service I was referring to," I said. "Getting you this tape. It's what you wanted, isn't it? It's what you searched Darryl Jackson's apartment to find. It's what you were so afraid the cops would get their hands on.

"Well, they didn't. I kept it from them. And now I'm bringing it to you. That's the service, and I want to be paid."

He looked at me a long time.

"So," he said. "That's what this is. Blackmail."

"Certainly not," I said. "I'm a reputable private detective. I've done some work and I want to be paid for it. I defy you to tell me I haven't done you a service. I did you a service and I want to be paid. I want $20,000."

He stared at me. "You're out of your mind."

"No, I'm not," I said. "Frankly, it ought to be fifty. I was gonna ask fifty, but then I'm just a nice guy. And fifty's too much for you to raise easily without making waves. I figure you can handle twenty all right."

He stared at me. "Who the hell *are* you?"

"That's not important," I said. "All you need to know is I'm a guy who did you a service who wants to be paid."

He thought for a moment. "All right," he said. "Fine. Now listen. I thank you for bringing me this tape. It was probably your duty to do so. You were right to bring it to me and not to the police. A public servant is under certain scrutiny, and in order to do his job effectively and serve his constituents, he has to maintain a certain image, and adhere to standards more strict than those enforced upon the general public. So what you've done is of some value.

"But $20,000 is out of the question."

"No, it isn't," I said. "It's peanuts compared to what Darryl Jackson was shaking you down for. And it's not blackmail. No one's gonna bleed you white. This is a one-shot deal. You're paying me for a service. As I said before, when I walk out of here you're never gonna see me again."

He took the tape and slipped it in his desk drawer.

"Frankly, I see no reason why I should pay you anything at all," he said.

"I was afraid you might have that attitude," I said. "But I have worked hard on this case, and I don't intend to take a loss. In the event you do not wish to pay me for my service, I have copies of this tape for channels 2,

4, 5, 7, 9, and 11. It will be interesting to see which station pays me most. It will also be interesting to see which one has the most guts. I don't know how much they can show on TV. Some of 'em may black out half the screen. Others may go with a small black rectangle. I don't know, but it will be fun to find out."

"But this isn't blackmail," he said sarcastically.

"Certainly not," I told him. "I did you a service and I want to be paid."

"Oh stop saying that!" he said irritably. "All right. All right. Obviously, I don't carry $20,000 on me."

"I know that," I told him. "I'll take a check."

He looked at me incredulously. "You'll what?"

"I trust you. You're an honest man. I'll take your check."

"A blackmailer taking a check?"

"I told you this isn't blackmail."

"Yes. You did."

He opened his desk drawer and pulled out a checkbook.

"Fine. If that's the way you want it."

He opened the checkbook. Took out a pen.

He looked up at me then, and despite his predicament, there was a note of triumph in his eye.

"All right, wise guy," he said. "You think you're so damn smart. I can't make this out to cash, you know. After working so hard to remain anonymous, you're gonna have to give me a name."

"I can't help that," I said. "You can't have everything."

He took the pen, poised it over the checkbook.

"All right, wise guy," he said. "How shall I make it out?"

I waited until he looked back up at me before I told him.

"Make it out to Matilda Mae Smith," I said, "of Jersey City, New Jersey."

43

I RODE THE SUBWAY HOME. It was rush hour, and I was strap-hanging in an unmercifully crowded car, but I didn't care. I was feeling pretty good.

I was glad I got the money for Matilda Mae Smith. The Congressman shouldn't have got off scott free. And the law couldn't touch him. There was nothing Mac-Aullif could do, not without those tapes, and I couldn't give them up. Not with Pamela Berringer in them. So it was right he should have to pay. It wasn't enough, but it helped.

And I couldn't have taken the money for myself, much as I need it. Then it would have been blackmail. The way I saw it, this wasn't. It was paying off a debt.

I suppose you could say I had an ulterior motive for giving the money to Matilda Mae Smith. You could say giving the money to a black woman was a gesture made by a disillusioned liberal to ease his conscience for the guilt he felt over the fear he felt about going into certain black neighborhoods. You could say that, and you'd probably be at least a little bit right.

'Cause the sad truth is, life is hard. And the older you

get, the harder it gets. And the things that seemed so cut-and-dry when you were young just aren't so easy anymore.

The thing is, the world's not perfect, and people aren't perfect, and you aren't perfect, and all those intellectual moral values that were so simple in college just don't work in the outside world. You have to do the best you can.

So, if you want to think of Matilda Mae Smith's twenty grand as conscience money, well fine, I can live with that. Perhaps it is. Perhaps I had selfish motives in wanting it for her. The thing is, I don't care. Whatever the reasons, it was the right thing to do, and I'm glad I did it. I feel good about it.

And I'm pretty pleased about how the case turned out, too. True, I had confronted X, and he knew who I was, and I didn't much like that. But MacAullif had assured me that X was going away for a long time, and the way I figured it, MacAullif's word was as good as I could get.

And the nice thing was they probably wouldn't even need me as a witness. After they'd taken him in, X had confessed. As Linda said, he was dumb. He bragged about it.

The cops had it all. How he had let himself into Darryl Jackson's apartment while he was out, appropriated the knife, waited in ambush, and killed him when he returned at a quarter to one. He'd gotten out of the building just before Celia Brown took up her position on the steps. Just before the Skirt came, found Darryl Jackson dead, and ransacked the apartment looking for something. Before the Parka came, and either found Darryl Jackson dead, or didn't go in at all.

Just before Gray Hair came and trashed the apartment too.

One of those three, MacAullif figured, probably excluding the Parka, had found and destroyed the book of johns. Because X hadn't taken it from Darryl Jackson. He said he hadn't, and he had no reason to lie about it, since he was confessing to everything else. He really was dumb.

And one thing you can be damn sure of, X didn't confess before MacAullif had advised him of his constitutional rights. It was a clean collar. There were no two ways about it. X was going down.

I felt mighty good about that.

And Pamela Berringer was off the hook. She and dear old Ronnie would probably be reconciled, whether or not they ever acknowledged to each other that she knew that he knew that she knew, etc., etc.

And the car pool would continue, at least for this year. And Tommie would play with Joshua, sometimes at our house, and sometimes at theirs.

And Pamela Berringer would be just another housewife again, just as if it had never happened.

I'm just not sure how I feel about all that.

Hall
  Murder.

C.3

Detroit City Ordinance 29-85, Section
29-2-2(b) provides: "Any person who
retains any library material or any part
thereof for more than fifty (50) cal-
endar days beyond the due date shall be
guilty of a misdemeanor."